Vig.
The Life of
Victor 'Vig' Green

DAVID LYONS

First edition.

Rue,

Hope you enjoy
reading this (or at least,
enjoy parts of it!!)

Cheers

CONTENTS

FOREWORD

This is a Las Vegas novel. I don't mean a gambling novel, because the essence of Vegas has never really been about the bets. That glittering oasis that arose out of the desert has always been more about the people who came. And just what kind of people they were.

Las Vegas is for those who never could be anywhere else. No matter what capital corner of America in which you were born and raised, the ones who came to Vegas quickly knew that they had to go. Didn't belong in the buttoned-up shirt and picket fence life where the rules were always written on the wall in indelible ink. Vegas is for those who judge by their own.

Morality is a funny thing. I'm no priest and you won't find me engaged in lectures about right and wrong. No worries if you have none, and if you do want some you can always follow the herd. But the pioneers of Vegas had ethics as firm as the Rosetta Stone. Not rule books and Sunday School conventions about evil and good. Their ethics.

"If it bothered me, I wouldn't have done it," Benny Binion often said. "Fact of business, I'm well capable of looking after my own." Binion didn't need God or the law to tell him what a man could do.

I was a Stardust man. And my first Vegas touchstone was a poker dealer there named Chuck Brock. Chuck had arrived in Vegas in the fifties or the sixties, when he was, "just a kid full of vinegar and piss. I didn't give a shit about nothing or nobody," he told me and the Luma Kid, us wide eyed and nineteen years old, with Chuck sitting at one of those school desk seats in the back of the sportsbook, making his baseball bets in the morning before going on shift at 11am. Chuck wasn't a great gambler, actually he was pretty damn poor, and he favored the nine or ten team parlays that were going to turn ten dollars into 100 grand when they hit.

That summer was my first long stint in Vegas. The Luma Kid and I took a Greyhound bus from the east coast to play low stakes Texas Hold'em on five hundred-dollar bankrolls with a shared room in the back of the Stardust motor lodge. We paid the eighteen dollar a night poker rate and availed ourselves of free food coupons for the snack bar and buffet. Everyone knew we were underage kids but at the Stardust we were allowed, according to the rules of that realm.

I can't remember where Chuck came from, but it hardly mattered. He had come to Las Vegas as soon as he was able, because wherever he came from couldn't hold him in. Like so many who made it to Vegas in those years, the square life wasn't his. And what made Chuck special, like Vig and Gina and so many I've known, was that despite being a rebel in every sense of the word, he had a moral code that he stuck to with a passionate pride.

The Stardust poker room of the late 1980s, right around the time that our hero Vig Green came to the desert, was a shell of its former renown. Once the biggest poker room in town, the opening of the Las Vegas Hilton and then the Mirage saw the Stardust room reduced to a modest size. But what the Stardust still had no other room could match, and that was the Vegas denizens that staffed it and dealt the games. The youngest among them had been there twelve years, and most more than twenty. They were a glorious crew of miscreants, cutups, and misfits, each with a name tag that also identified the place to which they would never return.

But Vegas took them in, and the wonderfully seedy Stardust was one of the most caring families in which I was ever involved. Yes they dealt in vice, in gambling and drugs and cons of the game, but to call them bad people is to not understand that most people are so uncomfortable with lawlessness precisely because they have no confidence in creating their own.

Chuck took the Luma Kid and I aside and said under no circumstances were we allowed to play in the stud hi-lo game that ran at the back of the room, where old man Joe and Billy the Kid were regularly engaged in cheating unsuspecting tourists out of their vacation dough. Billy the Kid was one of the top card mechanics in town. The poker room was mostly on the square. Cheating was regulated but not banned, and it was ok to cheat certain people at certain times. That was their law. And they did draw a line.

The mantra that the customer is always right did not apply in the jungle. Once a regular got upset at a bad beat and winged a chip rack in the dealer box straight at Chuck Brock. Chuck dived over the table and decked your man with a punch to the head. And he didn't stop there. Chuck was back at work the next day but the customer was gone. Those were the rules of the Stardust family. You had better be careful when cursing your luck.

Like Cully from Mario Puzo's great novel Fools Die, Vig Green is a hero for those Vegas days of yore. And one thing I will say about Vig, and Gina too. You can judge them for yourself and judge them how you like. But I'd have welcomed them as my own. Don't mistake Vig and Gina for anything but heroes. They are Las Vegas pioneers of the steel-coated marshmallow kind.

Jesse May, April 2020

1 ABE

Vig first visited Pahrump in August 1969. At the time it was a tiny little outpost town about sixty miles west of Las Vegas, and NV160 was the only paved road in the area. Once you left town the road was just a simple strip of asphalt in the middle of the desert. The ubiquitous blackbush and creosote bush served to underline the blandness rather than provide any break from the monotony. The August heat also meant that the distant Nopah mountains to the south, and Mount Charleston to the north, were barely distinguishable on the horizon.

The only thing notable about Pahrump at this time was that it was the closest town to Vegas that was technically located outside Clark County. In Nevada, brothel prostitution was legal, except where the county in question had a population of over twenty-five thousand people. This was a weird law that meant that all the bachelor parties abandoned the strip and crossed the county line to legally get their rocks off. Because of this traffic up and down NV160, the limousine drivers made a killing. In Las Vegas, four guys could ride around for a night in a limousine for the price of a couple of cab rides. Even if you didn't want to make the round trip to Pahrump, an extra few dollars could get you a couple of strippers to serve drinks in the back of the limo. If you were selective, the girls would also do a little escort work on the side. Most guys preferred to subscribe to the myth that the girls choosing to dance for money were honest wholesome girls saving up for beauty school, but once you spent any time in Las Vegas the line between dancer, stripper, and working girl got blurred very quickly.

Vig was travelling in the passenger seat of a one-year old Lincoln Continental driven by a gambler by the name of Abe. He did not know Abe particularly well; they had met a few times at fights that Vig had worked at in and around San Diego. Abe was hoping to strike it big in Las Vegas just before his divorce. Once he was divorced under California law, half his money would go to his ex-wife anyway, so if he won some cash on this final trip, she would never see it. If he lost all of 'their' money he could rightfully claim poverty in the settlement. He figured that he was freerolling. It was a cynical but mathematically sound plan.

The reason they had stopped in Pahrump was so that Abe could telephone his lawyer; he claimed that he wanted to give him one more shot to talk him out of it. He used the phone in a small bar on the southeastern edge of town. The first working phone had only been installed about five years previously, and it clearly had been well used by locals and passers-through alike. There was a sign above it that read; "Ten cent calls cost a half-dollar. Show your bail bondsman card for discount". The sign was famous, both for the markup and for the fact that it was used by every bail bondsman who made a pickup in Clark County... at least those who were heading east.

Vig had spent some time pondering his own reasons for travelling to Las Vegas. In his line of work, it was somewhat surprising he hadn't travelled there sooner, and he couldn't recall the specific event that had motivated him to finally visit. Once he had mentioned the idea to a couple of his business acquaintances, an opportunity had presented him with a chance for an open-ended and potentially lucrative visit.

Las Vegas had started out as a refueling stop for freight trains travelling between Southern California and Salt Lake City, and it took twenty-six years from the incorporation of the town for it to legalize casino gambling. The movies and history books cite this as the main reason for the success of the nascent city, but in the same year that gambling was legalized the residency requirements for divorce were cut to just six weeks. It went from a one-street town... to a one-street town full of sawdust joints where the people who built the Hoover Dam could come to swap vig for thrills, while bitter couples could check into adjoining rooms in a boarding house and wait a month and a half to tell each other to get fucked permanently. Over time the sawdust joints had begun to be replaced with rug-joints, and the rug-joints had given way to 'properties', that phrase used to describe the sprawling hotels and casinos that had since become the defining feature in Las Vegas. They still served the same games and the same fayre; the only difference was the minimum stakes and the quality of the décor.

Vig wasn't new to the world of gambling but he hadn't spent much time in licensed casinos, so despite being thirty-five years old he felt excited like a first-time spring-breaker. He subscribed to the newsletters, he had a well-thumbed copy of Scharff's guide, he knew the odds, but he also needed to see Las Vegas for himself.

After the short stop in Pahrump, they carried on the thirty-mile journey into Vegas itself. A smattering of small low-slung buildings heralded the arrival into the city outskirts, then the first signs of tracked housing until they finally turned north onto Las Vegas Boulevard. Up to this point, you could still be in any desert city, until you saw the 'Welcome to Fabulous Las Vegas" sign, which even by 1969 had become regarded as a local landmark at the beginning of the strip.

The strip hadn't quite made its transition to the modern theme-park-movie-set hybrid that it would become, but in 1969 the skyline on the strip was already unique. From the road, it was a visually overwhelming sight of densely packed signs advertising liquor stores, gas stations, car rental services, motels, and every minute or so the sight was dominated by the huge signage advertising the next major hotel.

At the end of the 'new' strip - before you arrived downtown - was Circus-Circus, a property that had been open only a year. Part of the charm when it first opened was the fact that there was no hotel, just a casino. When the Teamsters eventually loaned the owners money to build the hotel, one of the conditions was that they could open a jewelry and gift shop run by a mobster. Notwithstanding this 'heritage'… it was still an impressive sight. The one-of-a-kind clown-sign stood out on Las Vegas Boulevard towering over the small VIP parking lot, and the brightly lit canopy over the door was impressive even at twilight.

They pulled up at the valet. Abe flicked the small lever on the driver's door that unlocked the passenger side and motioned for Vig to get out. As Vig stepped out, Abe abruptly broke his silence and asked him how much money he had brought with him. If he had asked while Vig was sitting in the car it would have been weird, maybe a little sinister.

"A little over five hundred dollars."

(Vig had ten times that but was not telling this guy.)

"Put thirty dollars aside for the cab ride back, you'll be broke."

"I will if you put some aside for your second divorce lawyer, she won't take credit."

Abe laughed as he pulled away. Vig looked around before heading inside past the crowds of people (Circus-Circus was still relatively new and had remained popular). As he passed through the door, the dry desert was replaced by cooler fragranced air.

Vig had telephoned ahead to the casino host and arranged a six-dollar nightly rate. This was a great deal – the same price as Motel Six - and got him access to the buffet each morning and evening. That would give him bed and board for a month for under two hundred bucks, assuming he stayed in town that long. He tipped the baggage guy, told him he didn't need his bag carried, and rode the elevator to his room.

It was a small out of the way single; the type of room given as a comp to a drunk or a minor mark that the house didn't want to leave. "Have a room on us and leave tomorrow after breakfast" sounded like a kindly gesture from a host but was a last-ditch attempt to get a temporarily lucky player back to the tables.

The room had a small bed, a bedside table with a lamp, and a small coffee table flanked by two basic upholstered chairs. This suited Vig fine. He dropped his bag on the bed. It contained two spare shirts and two pairs each of socks and u's, so he could clean up while working if need be. He knew he could get a suit dry-cleaned cheaply while he slept or hang it in the bathroom with the shower running for twenty minutes to freshen it up.

Vig checked his pockets and counted up his cash. His five-thousand-dollar roll was there to help him gamble and have a good time, but he also had work to do. He had a reputation as someone who could be trusted to move cash from point A to point B and not steal it or talk about it. This was a useful rep to have in a town full of gamblers.

2 SIDNEY

3570 Las Vegas Boulevard South
August 6th 1969

As a kid, Vig had once spent a short afternoon at a fourth of July celebration past-posting at a local school carnival. It was a family-themed event with various carnival games and distractions. The game that attracted his attention that day was a simple spin-the-wheel that sat between the coconut shy and the ring-toss. The operator of the game would call for bets, and the players – adults and children alike – would place bets with coins on six different colored squares on a flat white wooden board. Each square had different odds painted on it in white. Curiously, the odds had clearly been painted over a number of times, perhaps the operator adjusted them to suit the venue. Kids wouldn't care if the over-round on the wheel was two hundred percent, but perhaps the punters at a horse-racing meeting or football game would look for something a little better.

There was quite a crowd around the table, maybe two or three deep. If Victor kept a low profile at the corner of the table he could leave a nickel sitting on the corner, outside of the playing area, just out of sight of the operator. When the wheel slowed at the end of each spin, the crowd would lean in to collect their bets, and he could gently nudge the nickel onto the red square and collect at even money. He was smart enough to only do it when there were multiple nickels already on the same red square. It was a rush to beat the system, and this was back when a nickel was worth something.

Vig didn't know the name for it yet, but this was past posting in its purest form; placing a bet after the result is known. He never found out if the operator ever spotted him or not. It's possible that he had been clocked and the carnie decided to let it be rather than make a scene and risk the game ending, but more likely that he had no idea and was just happy to rake in his thirty or forty or maybe one-hundred percent edge.

By the time Vig made it to Vegas he had progressed quite a bit from carnivals and nickels and was already part of the West Coast gambling community. He had spent many years working in and around boxing and had naturally been exposed to poker and a variety of other types of gambling.

Back then, long before pay-per-view, the bigger fights would have an official purse and an unofficial purse. The official purse got taxed, the other money didn't. At first, Vig was the guy who carried the unofficial cash - the 'other money'. In the boxing world he was sometimes called an assistant-promoter and sometimes called a promoter's-assistant, but in reality, he was what was called the "number two runner". He was the guy who moved the unofficial cash before and after the fight. Of course, when you are carrying cash between promoters, trainers, and fighters and get to know them well, you begin to carry messages, and then they get to trust you, so they just start asking you straight out if either fighter will take a dive, ask you to carry debts, and ask you to settle bets. From that point, you are carrying the 'other-other money'. Then you get smart, and ask these cheating assholes for a cut, and start betting your cut money on the fix. Or skimming the odds and betting the skim on the fix. Or covering for them while they fucked each other's girlfriends. Boxers can be assholes.

Hustling and grinding out a living ringside like this was how Vig had made it to Vegas with five grand in cash, and he had people to meet because he was owed a lot more. The first of those people was Sidney Poitier.

As well as being a great actor – this was five years before he was knighted - Sidney Poitier was a poker player. He had money and talent. The only thing he didn't have at the time was hustle when it came to settle his gambling debts. Vig was collecting a marker that Sidney had written in California to a poker player that had no interest in chasing a celebrity around to collect. It had taken a little time for him to convince Vig to take the debt – he had a rule about collecting other people's debts (don't fucking do it) but in this case he made an exception because it was supposed to be an easy collect, and instead of the usual twenty percent fee it was offered at forty if Vig bought the marker outright. This means that he had purchased the right to collect a legitimate five-thousand-dollar debt for just three-thousand dollars. For a high-profile actor who is relatively easy to track down - and unlikely to try and kill you - it was not a bad price.

Vig had done his research and had planned his arrival to coincide with an event that he knew Sidney was attending. His agent was throwing a little soiree for his best clients, and another poker acquaintance who worked as a brush in Ceasers had tipped off Vig that Sidney was heading downtown early to play a little high stakes stud poker.

Vig pulled out the phone book from the drawer beside the hotel room bed and thumbed it until he found the number for the Ceasers Palace front desk. A few seconds dialing and he was through to the poker room. He was lucky enough to get his brush on the first try.

"Any sign of my client?"

"He's here right now, playing fifty-hundred stud."

"How deep is he?"

"About twelve grand."

Bingo. Vig had gotten lucky; his mark was in the room, and if he was sitting at the table it was certain he would have a lot of money right in front of him for the taking. He knew that this was the tricky part. "I need to take him south."

A pause at the other end. "For how much?"

"Five thousand."

"That'll be tough." (That was code for 'please bribe me') "I finish my shift in forty-five minutes. Do it before then. I'll tell the dealer to keep the box short."

Vig gently hung up the phone and sat back on the bed reflecting on his plan. He was essentially going to trick Sidney into paying Vig the five thousand dollars that he thought he owed some other guy, using the marker he had signed to guarantee repayment. This would simply be done by asking him to make change for a five-thousand-dollar chip while he sat at the poker table. Players regularly made change for each other, and it was likely that he would have several thousand dollars in thousand-dollar or five-hundred-dollar denominations in front of him. Vig would simply take the change he provided and stiff him the money.

You would think that something like that would incite someone to shout thief, or start a fight, or make a scene. But Vig knew people, and he was almost certain that Sidney wouldn't do anything once he saw the marker, because he ultimately wanted to keep in action. A welsher - even a famous one - does not get to play poker on credit and sometimes not even with cash.

Before Vig left his hotel, he checked the marker one more time and folded it carefully in his pocket. He headed back down to the front door and took a cab from Circus-Circus down to Ceasers. Once there he didn't waste time taking in the surroundings, he just headed straight for the casino floor.

Five-thousand-dollar casino chips were (and still are in some places) known as a 'chocolates' due to their recognizable brown color. Vig had his five thousand dollars in cash in a brand-new wrapped brick in his pocket but needed to change the cash for a single brown chip before the ruse. There was no line at the cashier window, and thankfully the cashier didn't raise an eyebrow when Vig asked for the big-denomination chip, she just ran the cash through the mechanical counter and asked him to sign a receipt. Easy.

It was just a short walk past the small cocktail bar, across ther floor to the even smaller poker room. It was quiet, but sure enough, Sidney was right there sitting bolt upright in the five-seat at a four-handed stud game with a couple of old-timers and another not-quite-so-old timer. Easy.

Vig looked over at the desk. The brush was still on shift, chatting to the floor, pointedly facing away from the stud game. Vig didn't pause, he just stepped over to the table and took a seat; the one-seat closest to the door. The dealer barely glanced up. Vig sat down carefully without pulling the chair too close to the table as he wanted to be able to make a quick getaway if need be. As he sat, he took out the folded marker and placed it in his left hand out of sight. The dealer and the other players were focused on the hand in question; a small pot being checked to the river. Vig waited until the end of the hand when the dealer began washing and riffling the cards, then took out the small brown chip from his right jacket pocket and looked at the dealer.

"Buy in for five?"

"Five large?"

"Yep"

He looked at the single brown chip in Vig's hand. It's still true that many of the casinos on the strip will take each other's chips and exchange them for their own, especially for regular players. The general exception was large chips due to the risk of forgery.

"One of ours?"

"Yep"

He glanced over at the brush, who was now watching the table. Vig looked over and held up the chip nonchalantly. The brush nodded and turned away.

The dealer looked back at Vig. "Good to go, but you are going to need to break it."

Vig looked at Sidney's stack. Just over thirteen thousand dollars in low denomination yellow, black and green chips.

Much easier for another player to break it than it was for the dealer to pause his dealing to make change, especially in a limit game where there was less chips changing hands per hand.

"Hey there, would you mind breaking this for me?"

Sidney spoke "No problem, what do you want?"

"Four in yellows, rest in hundreds."

He started counting out the chips, barely looking at Vig. Two yellow, two yellow, two yellow, two yellow, then two small stacks of five black hundred-dollar chips each. The poker room was quiet, but Vig could imagine the brush and dealer's eyes staring at him.

The counting finished. This was it. Vig reached over and stacked up his chips with his right hand and without pausing snapped open the marker with his left in a well-practiced motion, flat on the felt where the chips had been. The other players froze. The dealer looked between Vig and Sidney.

Sidney didn't flinch, just looked down. His eyes moved slowly across the piece of paper, like he was trying to remember where and when he'd signed it. Vig had a momentary flash of fear that it might be a forgery. Sidney's eyes moved to the signature and he smiled. He never looked at Vig, he just glanced up at the dealer and said "I can't be going south on these guys. I'll take another five." Before he had finished speaking Vig had stood up with his brown chip and Sidney's little stack of black and yellow chips, leaving the marker behind where he had placed it on the felt. No apologies or explanations were necessary. This was very much not Vig's first time, and undoubtedly wasn't Sidney's first time either.

One of the other players couldn't help stealing a glance at the marker... of course, he had signed it "Sidney Fucking Poitier".

3 BERYL

128 Freemont Street
September 8th 1969

In the various biographies of the legendary physicist Richard Feynman, it is clear that he became an expert at every aspect of Las Vegas lifestyle apart from gambling. He mastered meeting and befriending interesting characters, dating showgirls, general pick-up-artistry, and driving for local mobsters. At the same time, he was utterly unable to reconcile the one-point-four percent theoretical edge on the don't-pass line with the actual random walk that your bankroll makes when shooting craps.

Like Feynman, Vig realized that successful – i.e. professional – gambling was about targeting the prejudices, weaknesses, and financial situations of other people. If you could provide an opportunity for others to satisfy their prejudices or hedge their risk-aversion with a wager, you could take the mathematical best of it. There was a lot of money in Vegas which meant there was money to be made if you were smarter than average and could keep on the right side and keep your 'nut' – your monthly commitments - low. If you could enjoy the spectacle and avoid any leaks at the same time, you could make gambling work for you, and make Las Vegas work for you.

After the first few weeks of moderate hedonism, Vig began to get into a slightly healthier routine, and to think about getting back to work. He ended up dealing a little poker and blackjack privately during a couple of conventions, where they were happy to use unlicensed dealers who would work for tips only. He also ended up doing a little work for an old boxing contact. This was not your typical boxing contact; she was British, and she was a she. Beryl Cameron-Gibbons (Vig called her 'Miss C-G') had been a top amateur promoter in Britain in the nineteen-fifties, before topping off her career with two big Cooper fights and semi-retiring to Red Rock. She still flew over to England regularly to watch fights, and no doubt still had a piece of a few fighters.

Vig and Miss C-G had first met when he was bringing the other-other money up to a fight in San Diego back in the early-fifties. The fight ended up being robbed and everyone had been burned except Vig and Miss C-G. From that point on the two of them became a little more than business associates, but a lot less than friends. That's as good as it got for people in their line of work.

They met again - the first time outside a boxing club - in Fremont Street. It was in the steak house in the rear of Binion's Horseshoe, a sawdust joint that marketed itself for real gamblers, so that real idiots could feel better about making Jack Binion's lawyers richer.

"Still got a big appetite I see, Vig?"

That accent was unmistakable; she was the only woman who called him Vig in a London accent. He put down his fork and slowly turned around in his stool. She was quite a sight amongst the midnight Binions crowd. Despite spending most of her life behind a bar or in a gym she always dressed for business, day or night. Sensible leather square-toed shoes with a small heel – practical for staying on her feet – and a long black slender dress with a broad white lace collar. Her platinum blonde hair framed a smile.

They may not have been friends but Vig was genuinely

happy to see a familiar face.

"Miss C-G! You in town for a visit?"

"I just moved out here, to a little place west of town."

"All the way over here?" Vig was surprised "The glamour of the London gyms not enough for you?" Vig gestured to the seat opposite him, and she sat down and placed her purse on the table in front of her.

"Ha! Those gaffs are all either too cold, or too hot. Much more consistent out here." She seemed to ponder the air for a moment. "Drier at least. Anyway, I see that you have made it to Vegas at last?"

"Yep. Been here a month. Starting to get the hang of it."

"Broke yet?"

"Nope. I bought a few local debts before I came here and have lived off the vig, plus I've played a little poker. I was thinking of staying out here a little longer, maybe getting some steadier work."

"What kind of work are you looking for?"

Vig raised one eyebrow. "The kind where you get paid."

"Well, if I recall correctly you know how to spread pontoon. Do you fancy running a table at my house for a couple of nights?"

Vig pursed his lips but didn't reply.

"I'll take that as a maybe. I'm having a couple of private parties this week, hosting some of my new local friends and some visitors from back home. I've a guy who'll tap you out for a break every forty-five minutes or so, you'll be one of three dealers working two tables. I can't hire union dealers because it violates their gaming permit and could hurt my promoter license application."

Vig was delighted. This was the type of break that might broaden his horizons a little in this town. A little money, a few drinks, and more importantly, some new contacts. Perfect, as long as he didn't have to…

"And I'll need you to come over early to park the cars."

4 RED ROCK

Blue Diamond Road
September 10th 1969

M iss Cameron-Gibbons had sent a car to pick Vig up from Circus-Circus and take him straight out to Red Rock, and he arrived just before seven o'clock, just as the sun was setting. The car was not a limousine, but it was air-conditioned and comfortable. This was the easiest ride to work that he'd had in a long time.

Her house was set back off Blue Diamond Road, on a little crescent with four other equally large detached houses. There were already a few cars parked near the drive, probably her own and the other guys working this party. The outside of the place was nice, not garish, and it looked like it had plenty of room. Vig wondered how much money was coming to the party. It might turn out to be an interesting night after all.

Miss C-G was standing at the front door as Vig approached. She was already dressed for the party; the dress she wore wasn't that different to what he had seen her in earlier, but the jewelry was more elaborate and if the diamonds were real, it certainly suggested that the boxing business in England had been good to her. Despite the early hour she already had a highball in her hand. It was comforting to see that not much had changed.

"Thanks for the dig out Victor. There'll be about twenty more of your big American monstrosities showing up in the next hour or so. You can leave them on the lawn; I'll be getting it paved in a couple of weeks anyway. Anyone who shows up later than eight can sort themselves out, I'll need you inside then to prep the layouts. If any nosy neighbors come out to complain about the cars on the lawn just tell them to go to hell and try and remember which of the doorways they scuttle off to."

The car parking was uneventful. Most of the partygoers were dropped off by their own drivers, so once the drivers had unloaded their passengers, Vig told them to park around the block. A few more arrived by cab or towncar, and the dozen or so who drove themselves appeared to be in rentals. Only a few of the arrivals seemed to be real locals. Some of the drivers who parked their cars elsewhere walked back around the corner to wait outside Miss C-G's house, presumably in case their charges left early and wanted to split. A couple of them were clearly not just drivers, but muscle.

Vig had spotted one driver pull up in a smallish convertible with a petite dark-haired woman at his side. At first, Vig assumed that they were husband and wife driving themselves, but he dropped her at the curb without a word, left the engine running and walked her to the door, then after she disappeared into the house, he came over to join Vig for a smoke. He seemed to be in a mood to talk. "How do you know the hostess?"

Vig gave the same answer whenever he was asked that. "Old friends."

"From boxing?"

"Something like that."

"You're a little thin to be a fighter."

"I park cars." (true, at least)

"Yeah I'll bet."

"Who was your passenger? She a friend of the hostess."

"I guess so, if she invited her to the party."

"Who is she?"

Silence. A different approach was needed.

"You work for her?" A pause. He nodded.

"What does she do?"

"Minds her own business."

He smiled to make it clear he wasn't being an asshole; he just respected his passenger's privacy. Perhaps Vig would have probed a little deeper if he had known that before long, he would be on more than first name terms with the mysterious passenger.

Shortly after seven-forty-five Miss C-G sent one of the other dealers outside to bring him in. It was clear that everyone who was important already arrived. Vig nodded farewell to the other drivers and stepped through the large front doorway.

If the house was nice from the outside, it was breathtaking from the inside. Not because it was particularly huge or opulent, but it had been decorated with taste. The floor was an off-white parquet, the walls of the main downstairs area were hung with what looked like tapestries, and the furniture – mainly leather – was sunk into the floor in three different parts of the open plan living room. It was a place to have a party; in fact it was a place you could have three parties. Vig had only met her in a boxing environment; at fights, in dressing rooms, and very occasionally in bars afterward, and hadn't really thought about what her home would be like other than the bar that he heard that she had lived in in London.

The other dealer walked Vig to the back of the huge living room, where Miss C-G was standing smoking a cigarette in a long ivory holder.

"Thanks for the help with the parking, Vig. Come into the kitchen, I want to talk to you."

Vig followed her up three steps to the kitchen. It was surprisingly small and closed off from the rest of downstairs. It looked like it was seldom used, presumably Miss C-G ate out a lot. Maybe that explained what she had been doing in Binions.

"Okay Vig. I'll cut to the chase because I know you are a bloke who talks straight. I had a mechanic due to come and work here tonight but it turns out that too many people already know him and know what he is. That's why you are here."

Vig cursed to himself. "Why do you need a mechanic?"

"There's going to be gambling tonight, as well as a little business. I need one particular guest to lose a little chunk of money, either at the pontoon table or later if we can get a poker game going."

"Who are you trying to take?"

"That's not important now Vig, all in good time."

"Surely there are better ways to take money off a mark. Why the drama and the risk?"

She took another drag. "This one owes me money. It's not much – just north of four grand – but she's giving me the runaround and I need to get it back, and I want to get it back publicly, so the rest of these locals know not to take me for a soft touch."

"Four grand? Seems like a hell of a lot of trouble. What makes you think I can grift four grand, maybe she'll get lucky?"

"She's tight as a duck's arse and will just want to win a little – she'll martingale to just take enough to pay her driver."

"Martingale? Is she some kind of idiot?"

"In business, no. But in gambling, it looks like she is. I've had her watched in all the casinos on Fremont and one or two in Reno, and she doesn't play much, but she Martingales."

"Hold on. You said you wanted to do this publicly. Does this mean that you expect me to deal her a crooked game?"

"Not a crooked game. Just six crooked hands in a row."

Six crooked hands, just to make a point. Vig had a general rule; never do anything just to make a point. Nobody gives a shit about your point other than you. He might be willing to bend that rule in this situation, as he was doing this to get paid while Miss C-G was making her point. But this was still a very bad spot. Dealing crooked blackjack was no joke, even for an experienced mechanic. And you could certainly say that Vig was an experienced mechanic.

5 AILEEN

1628 El Centro Avenue
A Saturday in 1954

Vig had trained himself to handle cards in his late teens. Initially it was just to protect his money from the poker cheats around the gyms and pool-halls where he received the bulk of his formative education and the bulk of his formative money. He had tried to keep his skills to himself, but an incident in a game in the Hollywood Legion Stadium early one Saturday morning had changed things.

The Hollywood Legion, together with the Olympic, were the home of west coast boxing for much of the early twentieth century, with the Legion running boxing events every Friday night, and a poker or craps game running most nights after the lights went out.

Tonight's poker game had been running since the boxing card had ended. Vig was the only money-runner who was allowed sit in on the game, as anyone else who handled fight money could not be trusted not to put their bosses bag-money into the game (or get robbed). Art Aragon was the hottest ticket in boxing in Los Angeles around that time and was still celebrating the previous night's victory with his entourage elsewhere in the building. The game was down to five-handed, with Vig, Aileen Eaton, Benny Georgino, one of the losing boxers from the undercard, and another hanger-on.

Vig had played with Aileen before and she was rolled, solid, and ahead. This was Vig's first time playing with Benny, and he was also ahead and had effectively shut down for the night, not putting much at risk and seeming just to mark time until Art was done partying. The boxer was stuck, but apparently owed money by Aileen which no doubt she was fronting him just so he could lose it back to her. Vig was just about even. The hanger-on was well up, having busted two other players from the game earlier in the night in a single hand. The game had gotten big as a result, with everyone at least a couple of grand deep, even the stuck boxer.

After the big hand that had taken the game from seven players to five, Vig had begun to watch the boxer very carefully. He seemed to be winning more often on his own deal, which the odds favored but could be a sign of something fishy. The conversation around the table had slowed down since about four a.m., as the game had become a race between Vig, Aileen and Benny to stack the two remaining weak players.

The deal was back around to the boxer, and he scrambled the cards on the table as usual, boxed them, and began a standard riffle. Each time between the riffle he would slide out a block of cards from the middle of the deck and place it on the top, then cut the deck in the middle… once… twice… three… four times.

Most of the time when he was shuffling his eyes were on his hands, but Vig had noticed that this time his attention was not on the cards but he was looking at the other players while making conversation. This was not particularly unusual for a regular poker player; what was unusual is that it didn't slow down his execution of the shuffle.

Vig took a slow hit from his beer and used the distraction to study the boxer's hands more carefully. And there it was. When the boxer dealt normally, he had a loose mechanics grip on the deck, and pulled the next card forward from the front of the deck, sliding one to each player in turn. Now the fingers on the right hand had a noticeably tighter grip on the deck, and his thumb was crooked slightly on top of the cards. When he dealt a card from the deck, he was pulling it out and more to the left with his left hand, and the smallest three fingers on that hand were slightly spread.

Vig knew that this could only be for blocking the movement of the right-hand thumb, and the only reason that thumb needs to move is to deal seconds. Dealing seconds is the practice of simply dealing the second-from-top card instead of the topmost card. It is typically done when the cheating dealer is saving the topmost card for a specific player – usually themselves. This is a very effective way of cheating in stud games. A crooked player can simply clock the topmost card, and then decide when (or if) to give it to themselves or another player based on the visible upcards.

Cheating like this was – and is – rarer than people think. Every poker playing idiot who takes a bad beat begins to think they were cheated, but more often than not it is simply a better player taking their money simply and effortlessly. This was without a doubt professional-grade cheating. Either someone was desperate, or more than one person was in on it. Well, now Vig knew. So, what to do next? Calling out a cheat has consequences, whether you are right or not. Other players would realize you were a sharp, so invitations to play would start to dry up. It might not just be one person cheating you, what if others around the table were in on it, maybe Vig was the sucker they were all trying to fleece? It was a bad spot and he had to consider his options.

They were on third street and Vig had an eight in the hole with a seven doorcard, and he had just paired the seven. Aileen and Benny had folded a king and a four respectively, and the hanger-on had a ten and king of clubs showing. The last card on this street naturally went to the boxer, and he had just paired his doorcard and was showing a pair of eights. Three strong hands, with a smallish pot.

Vig wanted to be sure of his suspicions, and this might be

the hand to do it. With two paired doorcards it would look less unusual to be watching the deal more closely, so little subterfuge was needed. With the highest pair, it was on him to bet, and he figured a check was prudent. The boxer made a small ten-dollar bet, and looked up at the hanger-on, who was staring intently at his cards.

"What you wanna do?" the boxer growled

The hanger-on was clearly nervous. If he was even considering staying in, he must have paired the ten or the king. "Gimme a minute."

The boxer was getting impatient. "Sevens have just bet into you, so if you have a ten or a king in the hole, you are definitely ahead."

"Unless… unless one of you has a set."

"Unless one of us has a set. Now what are you going to do?"

Vig stayed silent during this exchange. Normally in a money game he would stop this type of bullshit; with a third player in this hand they shouldn't be doing this kind of coffee-housing. However, there was something fishy going on and he needed it to play out.

"I raise to sixty."

So, the hanger-on had something. Or was setting up a bluff. Or had had a fucking aneurism and was drawing two to a runner-runner straight or flush. So now Vig found himself facing down a raise in a hand that he could be way behind in against a possible bottom dealer. Not a good spot.

Rather than raise and face an ugly re-raise, Vig figured that he would call and get another shot at seeing the boxer deal. He tossed in the sixty dollars without a word. The action was back on the boxer. If he was cheating and had a king or ten stashed on top of the deck intended for the hanger-on, then he wouldn't raise and risk Vig folding, he'd call this street and deal him the clocked topcard. If he didn't have Vig beat, he'd either fold or - if he wanted to run a bluff - raise.

Standard five card stud strategy suggested that a good player who calls here had rolled up sevens a fair percent of the time. However, this was not a standard game, it ebbed, it flowed, it became less about the cards and more about the situation.

His voice was even. "I'll call it."

Vig used his empty left hand to push his stack of ten five-dollar chips into the middle and moved his right hand up to begin dealing. He tried to look like he was focused on the two-hundred-dollar pot but kept watching the boxer's hands closely. The boxer's grip on the deck remained firm; Vig watched to see the tell-tale sharp movement of the right thumb as it slid the topmost card out of the way to expose the corner of the next – but there was no unusual movement. The boxer simply took the topcard and placed it alongside the two upcards of the hanger-on.

It was the king of spades.

Did this mean that Vig had been mistaken all along, and he had not been dealing seconds at all? Had he backed into three-of-a-kind himself and was hoping that the paired king would induce the hanger-on to stack off? The boxer knew that in a straight game this card would shut Vig down unless he had happened to deal him a rolled-up set.

The next card to Vig was another king. The hanger-on snapped his head up suddenly and looked at the boxer. The boxer narrowed his eyes and quickly dealt his own fourth card – a blank three.

"Check."

Now that play did not make sense. You don't give two paired doorcards a chance at a free card to catch up on fifth street – you must make them pay. Something was going on here, and Vig was determined to find out.

"A hundred."

Vig tossed a single black chip into the middle of the table. This was not an outrageous bet into a two-hundred-dollar pot, but with his paired sevens on the door against a pair of kings and a pair of eights, it was either a large bluff or a stone-cold value bet. Vig wished that he knew which.

"I'll raise to two hundred."

The boxer was in the same boat as Vig; the raise was representing a set or two pair, especially a bet of only half the pot which was dying for a call or even a big bluff. The hanger-on looked dubious. He glanced at Vig, then down at his chips, then checked his down-card, then glanced at Vig again. Why didn't he look even once at the raiser?

"I'll… er… raise. I raise to five. Five hundred."

A five-hundred-dollar raise meant he had an unbeatable set of kings or believed his open pair (maybe two pair) was good. This was an unusual raise, especially after the check. This was back in the days when a check-raise was considered bad etiquette – especially in five card stud and draw.

Vig was now facing a raise of four hundred, with a grand and change in the pot. By this time, Benny had gone to smoke a cigarette – Aileen couldn't stand the smoke – so it was just the three of them in the pot plus Aileen seated at the table. She had sat up and began taking notice of what was going on. Vig couldn't tell if she suspected something was fishy or was just watching a pot get built and trying to learn a few tells.

Vig paused. He couldn't be representing a set – Aileen had folded the case king. She had folded it quickly under the gun, and maybe the hanger-on hadn't seen it – Vig barely saw it himself. The boxer had nothing better than two pairs, as Vig had the other king. This weak fucker was betting into two possibly made sets. What did he know? Maybe he had marked the deck and Vig somehow hadn't spotted it.

Then it hit him; it was a simple sandbagging. These two were working together. The boxer had held on to the king and dropped it on the hanger-on to make the sandbagging look cleaner, but the idiots had forgotten that a king was already folded.

Vig was pondering his options when there was a crash to his left – Aileen had apparently knocked her whiskey and soda on to the floor. She grabbed a couple of napkins and began patting herself down.

Vig's mind raced. For crying out fuck, was this part of the sandbagging? If so, it was the oldest trick in the book. Create a distraction and either clock a mark's hand or switch palmed cards into your own hand. Did Benny know something, and was that why he had ducked out?

"Gimme a hand here kid." She was on the floor.

He paused. He hadn't taken his eyes off the cards, and wasn't in any hurry to.

"Goddamn it, grab some napkins and help me mop this up."

It looked like Vig had no choice. "OK you guys, no stealing my king!"

The hanger-on's eyes bulged, and he looked at the boxer. The boxer wasn't laughing.

Vig grabbed some napkins from his side of the table and began cleaning up. The glass hadn't shattered, just broken into three pieces and the ice and booze was spreading under the table. Vig reached down to help her, but she seemed to have most of it already taken care of and had a large wad of napkins in her hand. What had she been yelling for?

"They'll do you no good, use one of these."

She passed Vig a napkin and the first thing that he noticed was that it was folded perfectly diagonally in two. The second thing he noticed was that it had something small and white concealed in it. He used his right hand to reach over and take the napkin, and briefly slid it open to see what the white thing was.

It was the seven of diamonds.

He didn't even pause, just quickly moved his left hand down to the floor and pretended to mop up some of the booze. After a few seconds the commotion was over, and he was back in his seat.

"Looks like we're done. What was the action?"

"As if you forgot. Four hundred on you." The boxer sounded impatient.

Aileen was also back in her chair, patting herself down. Vig looked over towards the door, and there was Benny standing in the doorway with his eyes fixed on the game. Vig didn't know exactly how long he had been standing there. The napkin with the concealed card was still in Vig's right hand. In the four seconds that had passed he had already made his decision; the timing would have to be perfect.

"Well I guess somebody thinks I have a good hand, so I'll bet it. I raise another fourteen hundred."

Vig reached over with his left hand, angled his fingers downward, and began pushing a stack of twenty black chips into the middle with the back of his hand.

The boxer licked his lips "You can put in an even two grand if you want."

"No, just your four and my fourteen is fine."

Vig had pushed the top of the stack a little far and it toppled forward into the pot, so he made a show of lifting the napkin up and dropping it cleanly on the table, and swiftly reaching out with his now-empty right hand to catch the toppling stack. He was too late, and the chips splashed in front of him. Vig moved to restack them with both hands, eventually bringing two stacks of ten chips together and pulling the top chip off each one. He flicked the chip from left to right, and then as he flicked the two chips back into his right hand, grabbed the napkin between his left thumb and forefinger, but instead of taking the napkin with the card, he grabbed the face-down eight with the napkin and yanked it cleanly away, letting the face-down seven slide out from the fold in its place.

Vig didn't even know who was looking at him while he made this move. The boxer could have spotted it, but Vig believed that he had been careful enough, and the chip-flicking distraction had worked. Also, the boxer had no reason to suspect the reintroduction of palmed cards as he'd scrambled and riffled the deck carefully himself, and a mechanic worth his salt would have the deck counted down on their own deal at the very least. The hanger-on seemed to be more focused on the boxer, and Aileen... well Aileen was probably curious to see if Vig would introduce the card. Benny had begun to walk back over to the table; who knew what he knew?

This changed the hand significantly. Vig now had rolled-up sevens with an unpairable king kicker. He replayed the hand to himself in his mind; would his play so far be plausible with the cards he was now holding? The boxer had a pair of eights and a three showing, and the hanger-on had a pair of kings and a ten showing, with both of the other kings already out.

Vig took a slow, measured breath. Apart from the cards on the table, he also had an eight wrapped in a napkin in his pocket that he needed to get back into the deck – but first things first.

"How much behind?" the boxer asked Vig, as if he didn't know. He could barely conceal his excitement.

"About another five hundred in chips, and a grand in cash."

"Call. What about you?" he gestured to the hanger-on.

The hanger-on had a look on his face like he had no idea what the fuck was going on. These guys were confederates all right, but the boxer was the mechanic and the boss. It was clear as day now. Vig wondered what fifth street would bring in this little bit of theatre.

First card off the deck for the hanger-on was an ace; this left left him with two pairs of kings and tens, or maybe kings and aces in this crooked game. His eyes were fixed on his cards, almost like he was afraid to look up.

Second card off the deck was placed directly in front of Vig, and of course it was the case seven of clubs – he had an apparently unbeatable four-of-a-kind, but the boxer must believe it was a strong-but-not-so-strong three-of-a-kind. Before Vig had a chance to consider this, the boxer dealt himself his own final card, another ace. This gave him a pair showing, but most likely with a third as his downcard.

Action was on the hanger-on, and he clearly was way out of his depth. He must have had an agreed plan with the boxer but the whole hand had gone way off-piste. His hands were shaking, and he could barely get the word out.

"Check."

In this spot the boxer knows that Vig puts him on a made set of eights, and that Vig's trip sevens were behind. He could not be expecting Vig to bet his last fifteen hundred, and practically jumped when Vig did precisely that.

"You don't think I have the set?" he scowled.

Vig looked up at him, eyes off the table for the first time. "I think we both paired our doorcard."

The boxer couldn't help himself – he glanced over at Aileen. She was sitting there with a thin smile on her face. He looked doubtful just for a second, but then his face cleared.

"You think he has the other seven, Aileen?"

"You know I don't coffee house."

"You only say that when it suits you. I call."

He didn't even wait to see what the hanger-on (who had a couple of hundred behind) was going to do. He called, and flipped over his eight to show his trips.

Vig tried to be as casual as possible when he turned over his seven. But not too casual, it was a big hand and a big pot, and probably was going to be the last one of the morning.

"Looks like I got lucky."

The boxer looked at the card, disbelieving, eyes bulging. He reached over and rifled through the sevens, counting them as if to be sure there was four. His next move depended on whether he had stacked the deck or not and knowingly given Aileen the seven, or whether Vig had indeed gotten luckier than he had planned for.

He stared at Vig, then his gaze turned to Aileen. His hand reached down to the muck of folded cards in front of her.

"Stop." The voice was sharp and echoed around the empty hall.

Everyone froze.

It was Benny. He was standing, legs apart facing the table, directly between it and the door, and he had his right hand held casually inside his jacket. His voice was measured but carried across the empty hall. "What card are you looking for, friend?"

"This kid... this kid cheated. He couldn't have had quads."

"Why not, exactly? You saying you didn't deal him a seven in the hole?"

"He cheated. This is bullshit. I'm not paying."

Aileen spoke up "You can pay now, or I can have it taken

from your next purse. That is, if you ever get to fight in this time zone again."

The boxer motioned as if to draw back his hand for a hit, then looked around him and thought better of it.

"This kid has cheated me."

"Nobody has cheated you." She spat the words out in clipped tones. "You stacked the deck like a fucking two-bit carnival barker, and you couldn't even get that right."

The boxer opened his mouth to speak but she cut him off.

"Here's what's going to happen. You can hold on to your last five hundred, and your boyfriend here can hold on to his last two hundred. If you feel that is not enough, or not fair, you can take this discussion outside with Benny. Or indeed, with Art. I'll see you" – she pointed at the boxer– "at your next fight in two weeks. I'll see you" – she pointed at the hanger-on – "never again in my life."

There was a beat. Neither the boxer or the hanger-on budged.

Aileen screamed "What are you two waiting for? GO!"

The shout echoed around the hall and reverberated amongst the stacked seats and sawdust. They both jumped up and ran for the door.

Benny shouted after them "I'll be eating breakfast at Jim's on the next block in ten minutes. I don't want to see either of you there."

Benny turned back towards the table. A little more relaxed, but still with his hand in his jacket.

Aileen's attention then turned to Vig.

"Now what do we do with you, young mister Green?"

Vig then realized that this hadn't been a favor. She knew that he'd made them as cheaters, and she had only palmed him the card to see if she could send them both off broke in a single hand. Vig knew this was probably not life threatening but was wondering would he get to keep any of the money in front of him. He didn't have long to wait.

"You're a good kid, you've seen this sort of shit before, right? You brought a thousand of your own, so you can take that with you, and … let's see… how about the same again. Two grand seem fair to you?"

Aileen's stoic poker face had dropped, and she was being businesslike and friendly, like she was offering a cigarette. As Aileen spoke, Benny had slowly walked up to the table and was looking down at Vig, almost amused. Both seemed to be waiting for a response, but not particularly interested in what the response was.

"Don't forget that if I hadn't slipped you that seven, you'd be broke."

Vig's options were very clear. He nodded.

"One more thing. You are not welcome in any poker game at any of my fights, or against any of my fighters, or in any game in which I am playing. Or any game I might be playing. You may or may not be the world's only honest mechanic, but I don't care to find out. Those two idiots are going to tell the world how they were sharped out of their money by a kid from the west coast boxing games, and that's fine by me. But they're also going to hear from me how I blacklisted you from the poker games in the west coast, and let you go home more or less intact. I realize this fucks you over a little, but that's why you're getting to keep my two grand."

More or less intact? HER two grand? Vig bit his lip.

"Spend the money wisely. I'll see you next weekend no doubt. I'll be gracious and polite; as will you."

And that's how Vig's career as a card mechanic was cut short. The next time he'd manipulate cards for serious money would be over fifteen years later in Red Rock, and that would end up just as messy.

6 GINA

Blue Diamond Road
September 10th 1969 (late)

"You've got a thirty-minute break."

The words were spoken at the same time as the tap on the shoulder. Vig had dealt two thirty-minute downs on each blackjack table, and so far it had been quiet. He guessed that nobody had come to the party early just to gamble, they were too busy mingling, or catching up, or getting outside the cocktails.

The two card tables were set in a large alcove on the bottom level of the living room, with the dealers' backs to the wall. It seemed like there may have been a bar here before, with deep marks on the carpet as if heavy furniture had been moved.

Across the other side of the room was a long, high, table made of either real stone or very convincing Formica. It seemed to be serving as a temporary bar. One end of the table held twenty or thirty bottles of liquor arranged in rows, with the bottles at the end of each row topped with a pourer. On the other end of the table were the same number of bottles of red wine. The rest of the table was covered in empty wine and highball glasses. Two older guys stood behind the bar serving drinks to order, with one of them occasionally disappearing to replenish the large half-barrel of ice.

As he crossed the floor, Vig saw a couple of faces that he recognized from the Los Angeles and San Diego boxing scene. One or two of them noticed him and nodded a brief hello; presumably nobody thought it was particularly strange that a boxing promoter would have a known money runner dealing blackjack at her new Las Vegas home. There were also some people he vaguely recognized from television, but no face he could put a name to.

Nobody looked like they could be the mark, at least not that Vig could tell. He took the few steps to the small kitchen that was now effectively serving as the staff breakroom. Miss C-G was there, holding a drink.

She didn't wait to be addressed. "You spotted her yet?"

"Nope, don't think so."

She looked into her glass, rolling the ice around. Vig thought it looked like she was trying to delay pouring herself another one. "How's the table going?"

"Fine. You got some rollers here."

"Are they tipping you well?"

"The winners are, but there aren't many of those."

She smiled. "Good. Don't bitch about the run of the cards to me. I'm not giving a mechanic a percentage of the drop in my own house, and I know you are not stupid enough to deal them winners to hustle for tips. By the way, you don't have to share your tips with the other dealers if you don't want to."

Vig said nothing.

Another drag from the cigarette. "So, your float is still healthy?"

"Yep, healthy."

"Okay. Your mark is here, and she is currently walking around with a cut man who flew over this week, sort of … showing him around town."

Vig laughed. "You are setting her up with a cut man?"

She didn't find it funny, or at least didn't show it. "Pete's a perfectly nice guy, with more manners than most who hang around ringside. Anyway, it'll make her easy to spot."

Vig poured himself a coffee and sat on one of the high stools that were pushed up against the counter.

"Are you really sure that you want to go through with this?"

"Sure as shit, sunshine."

"One last question. I presume this mark plays more or less basic blackjack strategy? It makes it much harder to stack a deck if she splits tens or doubles twelves." He thought for a second. "What if she plays two boxes?"

"Don't fret. She'll play you one box right off the card."

"Good."

Vig waited the remaining fifteen minutes to his next down, finished his coffee, did a little preparation for the main event, checked the line of his jacket, and went back out into the living area.

While they had been talking, the party had seemed to have gotten a little busier. It had certainly gotten noisier. One of the blackjack tables now had a female dealer in the box and six players seated. The other - where Vig was scheduled to take over - had the other male dealer in the box with two guys sitting in the middle seats talking but not playing.

When Vig stepped to the side of the quieter table and tapped the dealer on the shoulder, he barely looked up, just took a couple of steps back to let him slide into the box.

It occurred to Vig that this was probably as good a time as any to try and find out a little more about what was going on. He whispered to the dealer "I hope you haven't spent your tips already."

That got his attention. "We're splitting the tokes, right? That was my first shift tonight and I haven't even dealt a dozen hands yet."

Vig laughed. "Maybe, but with no boxes who knows how much she's pocketing?" He gestured to the other table, where the pretty dealer was sharing a joke with some of the players at the table. She certainly was better looking than the average blackjack dealer on Fremont.

The other dealer saw the look on Vig's face and guessed

what he was thinking. "If you are wondering, she was fired from the Dunes for partying with players after her shift." He didn't elaborate, just gave an attempt at a knowing look and walked back to the kitchen.

Vig took a few moments to check out the setup. The table was smaller than those you would typically find in a Las Vegas casino but heavy and well built. There was a large and almost-full chip case set into the dealers' side, a small chrome L-shaped box for the mucked cards on the right. A small shelf under the table had plastic-wrapped decks of cards, about a half-dozen each of red and blue. Typically, there would be a slot set into the table with a box underneath to catch the tips, but this was missing from this table; it probably meant that Miss C-G had brought them over from her place in England. Satisfied, Vig began to wash the deck that the previous dealer had left fanned out on the felt. As soon as he had finished the wash and had begun to riffle the cards, the two players seated at the table stopped their conversation and turned their attention back to the table. He gave them a friendly smile "Ready to play, gentlemen?"

"Now that he's gone, I think we are."

"You boys didn't have any luck with him?"

They exchanged glances. "We know him from the Palms."

"Let's hope I can get the cards to fall your way."

The player on the left smiled, looking straight at Vig. "As long as you deal from the top."

Vig tried to keep the nervousness out of his voice. "All from the top, sir."

What the fuck? Who says that at a blackjack table, even at a private party? Vig couldn't believe that Miss C-G would bring these guys in on it for some stupid reason. He also couldn't understand why the other dealer might be ripping these guys (or anyone else) off by dealing seconds. Had she brought her 'old friend' in as a backup mechanic?

It was a single deck game; easy enough to deal but also easier to fix than a multi-deck shoe game. These two guys were playing dimes and quarters (ten-dollar and twenty-five-dollar chips) and playing pretty close to the card. Vig kept his dealing slow and measured, and kept his grip loose, to keep any heat off. How in Christ's name was he supposed to bust the mark with these two guys suspecting a hooky game, and with the other dealer mixing it up at the same time, and Tits McGee making goo-goo eyes at the players at the other table and openly hustling for tips?

Vig told himself the next time he saw Miss C-G he'd ask for a break, and either confront her about what the hell was going on or just get out of there. However, before he got the chance three women approached his table. It was Miss C-G herself, with her left arm linking a slim and attractive woman in her thirties in a relatively modest evening dress, and her right arm linking a much younger but equally attractive girl, who was carrying what looked like two whiskey sours. They approached the table; the seated men looked like they were expecting them.

"You guys broken my bank yet?"

"Nobody could break your bank Beryl!" this was the younger guy on the left.

"I've found your two companions gossiping in the sunroom, I figured you might need the luck."

"Let's hope they weren't plotting against us." this was the older guy on my right.

The younger girl stepped forward "I brought you guys drinks."

"Great. Just in time. We are just getting warmed up with the new guy." lefty nodded towards Vig and slipped his arm around the younger girl, motioning her towards the empty stool.

Miss C-G laughed and responded. "I'm sure he'll be lucky for you. He's an old friend, aren't you?"

Vig looked up at her, and their eyes briefly met. "Old friends." He smiled and held her gaze for a second.

"If he knows how to double-paint a two, then we're all good." this was the older of the two women, who had moved to a stool at the other end of the group. She was looking straight at him.

Vig didn't match her gaze "Just over nine percent of the time."

She smiled "A dealer that knows the odds. I'm not sure if that's a good thing."

Lots of women players smile at male dealers and lots of women players flirt with male dealers, and Vig thought for a second that he got a flash of something from the older of the two women. Fuck. Anyway, no time to think about that. He now had four seats filled, with a possible fifth, and no sign of the mark yet. He was getting frustrated, the more people at the table the more difficulty in controlling the game, more chance of being spotted, and more risk overall. Then Miss C-G dropped the bomb. She slid in beside the older woman on the left "You going to try and cut and run for a lousy hundred bucks as usual Gina? You know how Martingale died, right?"

So this women Gina was the mark.

Surely it didn't have to be right now? Miss C-G couldn't expect him to deal six straight bust hands, with no time to set a deck, with Miss C-G plus at least two other sharp players watching. He started to get the feeling that maybe this 'Gina' wasn't the one being set up with an impossible task.

OK, it wasn't strictly impossible.

Vig had prepared two decks during his break and now stood with one on each inside pocket. One of them was pre-set with six consecutive winning (for the dealer) hands at the top, the challenge with that one was to ensure that the wash, shuffle, and cut between hands didn't disturb the order of the top half of the deck. The only problem was that it would only work heads-up.

The second deck was a little cruder, and Vig had only put this one in place in case of emergencies. The bottom eight cards of this deck were two fours, two fives, two sixes, and two sevens, and two aces were sitting at the top. Bringing this complicated fucker into play would in theory enable him to pretty much deal himself a nineteen or twenty or even a twenty-one as needed multiple times in a row, by pulling the right card off the right place at the top and bottom of the deck;

bottom dealing was arguably easier in single-deck blackjack. In a pinch, he could switch in an ace downcard to make blackjack right off the bat. But this meant he had to deal thirds the entire rest of the game, and keep the order straight during the shuffles, and do all of this about eighteen inches from a few heavily invested and watchful players, and the house who may or may not want him to fuck it up. A fuckup would be embarrassing for Vig, but what would Miss C-G do if he blew it?

Vig decided that it was not going to be. He had to let Miss C-G know that this was too risky. He had also started to think that maybe the other two fuckup dealers were a smokescreen, so she could deny any knowledge if he was caught. On the other hand, she had clearly identified him as an old friend, so there was probably no wiggle room for either of them if something went wrong.

"I hope you are all going to give us plenty of action tonight! If the table gets quiet I'll have to take extra cigarette breaks, and my doc tells me I shouldn't smoke so much."

Miss C-G was having none of it. "No such luck from this motley crew. Gina will hit and run us, the two boys will count you down especially on a full table, and – sorry sweetheart I don't remember your name – well she just looks like she's stacked with beginner's luck."

"Her name's Melissa." the other woman snapped sharply, as if irritated by Miss C-G's lapse in memory. There was a beat, and the two guys looked at each other and shrugged.

Now Vig was not a religious person, but at that precise moment he was praying hard for a distraction to switch in the decks and boy did he get one. There was a yell from the other table, then the yell was joined by two or three other shouting voices. Everyone's head snapped around to see what was going on, everyone except Vig. He whipped his hand into his pocket, masking it with a straightening of his dress shirt. He swapped out the mucky deck in one swift movement as he grabbed the boxed cards and put them on a little ledge behind the edge of the table. Even if the old deck was spotted, it could easily be a spare; you'd need spare decks on a night like this with the cards getting more bent as the players get more drunk.

Vig needn't have worried. The commotion had turned into an argument, and rapidly looked like it was going to turn into a fight. The blonde dealer had been replaced by the young guy that he had spoken to earlier. He must have only dealt a few hands, but one of the men – a smallish but wiry guy – had reached across the table with both hands and was gripping the dealer's hand with the cards still in it.

"Let go of me, asshole."

"Beryl. Get your arse over here." he shouted in a thick British accent, no panic or aggression in his voice.

The dealer was still struggling and yelling. "LET GO OF ME."

But the wiry guy was not budging. There was another more well-built player at his side who looked like he was with him and looked like he was ready to cut up rough if needed. The table was full, with cards and chips strewn across the felt.

Miss C-G slid off her stool and moved quickly over to the other table.

"Don't let go of him Darren. What did you see?"

"Get this guy off me!"

"What did you see Darren?"

"Your little fucker" – he spat the word – "is dealing seconds."

"I'm NOT. You've no proof. Don't believe him Beryl. You know me."

"Shut up. Show me."

Miss C-G walked over to the table. The wiry guy yanked the dealer's hands over the table, lifting him off his feet without losing his grip on his hands. It looked like the dealer was trying to drop the deck, but this 'Darren' was having none of it.

"He's dealt a ten and then switched in an ace to himself twice. Clocked it the first time, wanted to catch him in the act the second. The ace is still in his hand."

"You've seen it."

"Nope. I just know it's there."

Miss C-G reached into the mass of knuckles and managed to wrench out the top card. It was the ace of clubs. She reached in again, lifting the hands above her head, and pulled aside the black cut card at the bottom of the deck. The dealer tried to look nonchalant and angry, but the mask was slipping and replaced with a combination of horror and panic.

"Another ace." She looked disappointed, as if she hoped that Darren had been mistaken. "Top and bottom."

The dealer's reaction was instant "This is bull, this is BULL! I didn't put them there. I deal a square game, you… you know that Beryl, right? You know me? There's four aces in the deck, they could easily have ended up there."

She considered this for a second. "I suppose you're right."

"VIG!" she lifted her voice above the hubbub, and suddenly the table went silent, and the silence spread out to the rest of the room. She was looking directly at Vig. As others started to realize who she was looking at, they also started to turn towards him. The last to turn their gaze to him were the players seated at Vig's table.

Once Beryl knew she had the room's attention, she spoke softly, casually, as if ordering a drink. "Vig. Can you please tell Darren and this piece of shit what the odds are for an ace to find its way to the top and another to find its way to the bottom?"

"The top is twelve to one. The bottom, that's another sixteen to one. That's exactly two-twenty to one for both."

She looked at the dealer, who was looking at Vig with a thin film of sweat on his face. "That's less than half a percent."

A voice from the crowd. "Hey what the hell, I'm out over a G!"

The voice was joined by a few others. Before the hubbub could get any louder, Beryl interjected with voice raised. "Folks. I'm going to make good on all the hands that dealer has dealt since the start of his down. It's only twelve o'clock. Just tell Charlie how much you're out, he'll square the total with the cash in the drop plus whatever we find when we search our friend here. Don't worry folks, I'll make you all whole, and we'll get the party started again."

Darren still had the dealer's hands gripped, but by this time he had stopped struggling.

She walked towards Darren but when she spoke to him she kept her voice raised, to ensure the crowd could hear "Take him to the garage and see if he's any cash in his jacket pocket, socks, or lining of his jacket or trousers. Ignore his wallet or billfold, he won't have had time to switch the money in there."

Darren – his grip still vice-like on the dealers hands - was almost disinterested at this point. "Then what?"

The dealers eyed widened. He looked like he was going to say something but thought better of it.

Miss C-G paused and let him take in the moment. She was speaking to Darren but looking at the dealer. "Nothing too rough. I've just moved here and have a license to protect. Just make it hard for him to deal pontoon for a while."

The five or six other players that had been sitting at the crooked dealer's table had scooped up their piles of bills and began crowding around Miss C-G. Before she began speaking to them, she turned to Vig and said "Sorry Vig, I'm afraid you'll have to cut most of your breaks and push through. I'll make sure you're looked after, just stick to the plan."

Stick to the plan. That meant she still expected him to go through with it. The more that Vig thought about what he was being asked to do, the more ridiculous it began to sound. Two crooked dealers out of three, plus a fired party-girl dealer, and the first crooked dealer was going to end up with what he could only assume was a set of broken fingers at least. He had no doubt that if he screwed up and claimed Miss C-G had put him up to it, she'd not miss a beat and just throw Vig to the wolves too. What else could go wrong?

He didn't have to wait long to find out.

"You know your odds. Here's a tip for luck."

The woman – whose name he now knew was Gina – had a folded twenty-dollar bill in her outstretched hands, and was smiling.

He couldn't help returning the smile. "Keep it. You might lose."

Her smile didn't budge. "I thought that was the idea tonight, but I'm not so sure now."

She turned to her companion, who it now seemed she didn't know that intimately. "Buddy, I'm sorry that Melissa's friend is running late. I'm going to go and find out what's keeping her, I'm sure you'll get on like a house on fire." The smile again, and she was gone.

Jesus, she was pretty. Vig had to get out of here.

"Beryl." – Vig had never called her that since he'd met her.

"Vig?"

"Beryl. I'm out I'm afraid."

"We had a deal."

"That was before the finger-puppet show. You wanted someone reliable, but it's clear your standards have slipped."

More firmly. "Vig. We had a deal."

"We did. But now, if you'll pardon the expression; this deal – and this dealer - are fucking off."

7 MURRAY

3535 Las Vegas Boulevard South
November 1st 1979

Vig had been driving Abe's Lincoln – no pun intended – and it had seen better days. They had bumped into each other at Denny's only a few months after the drive to Las Vegas. Abe had apparently succeeded in doing his wife out of her settlement; he claimed he had tipped almost as much as he had lost. He was happy despite being broke, and because Vig happened to be flush, the car changed hands. It had been Vig's faithful companion, and occasional office and apartment, for the intervening decade.

He was en route to opening day of the Imperial Palace. Actually, it was technically a reopening; the place was not new. It had opened as the Flamingo Capri motel, then in 1977 the new tower was added. The tower's name ended up sticking, so the property was rebranded, refurbished and was now being relaunched. As the new tower was set back from the strip, the owners wanted to make sure that they made a big impression to passersby, so they erected a marquee-style pagoda on the street frontage to catch attention. The strip was changing, and catching attention was the name of the game. Vig pulled up to the marquee and handed his keys to the valet, he recognized him from another hotel, they'd clearly hired in some extras for opening night.

Not much had changed inside other than the décor. They had gone all in on the oriental theme, and Las Vegas then, as now, transcended any accusations of cultural appropriation. They simply took a theme and ran with it from the light fittings, to the uniforms, to the napkins and the chips. It was not trying to be like the imperial palace in China, it was succeeding in being what everyone imagined an imperial-palace-themed-hotel-in-Vegas would look like. It was beyond style, beyond homage, beyond anything.

The owners of the I.P. (as it came to be known) didn't care what the critics or the culture vultures thought of the design. The people would vote with their bills and coins. It was still a few years before the entertainer Dave Swan would take the stage at the I.P., but he always expressed the opinion that the life of a comedian was like the life of a Vegas property.

"Comics and casinos don't worry about critics, because any criticism is too little too late. At the end of a set if the audience laughs, anything after that means nothing; they voted, and the results are in. For a new hotel as long as the cards are being dealt and the handles are being pulled then nobody gives a shit what the papers say."

The internal layout of the casino floor hadn't changed since the refurbishment, the main bar had always been called the Sake Bar and hadn't changed under the new brand. The barman – who hadn't changed either – was well known in Las Vegas. He was a young British guy called Tony who Vig knew from the local poker games (i.e. those inhabited by locals). He placed a bourbon in front of Vig without them exchanging a word.

Vig didn't make a habit of frequenting the same bars repeatedly but he made an exception for this one. He turned on his stool to face the casino floor. The groups of broke girls were sitting as usual at the penny slots feeding in brown coins in between trying to catch a bored waitresses' eye. Vig smiled; only pretty girls get away with that, or locals who know when the good spots were quiet and had more waitresses then they needed. The ubiquitous working girls could make a drink last an hour and wait to be bought another by a prospective customer. They saved their tips for the security guards. For the rest of us, ordering drinks in Vegas required a special skill. When you have money, and want to gamble, the temptation is to sit at a table, play, and wait for the waitress. That's a rookie mistake; the best strategy is to step up to the bar and get yourself a beer and bring it to the table. That means you aren't looking over your shoulder for the girl like some guy who rode the bus in for the weekend. Also, once your glass looks empty you have a better shot at getting a waitress to take your first order. When she does, tip her treble. That'll keep her coming and maybe even allow you to order two at a time. Older waitresses are the best for this approach… they want a dollar bill for every drink in every order. One night Vig had been shooting dice in the Flamingo with two sportsbook clerks he was trying to butter up. They ordered three beers and three daiquiris every round, and the waitress just stood at the table waiting for them to finish and reorder. A few bucks for six drinks a dozen times over, easiest two hours work for her and great value for her three value-hunting customers.

What sort of work requires Vig to be sitting in the bar in the I.P. at one o clock in the afternoon? Waiting. In his line of work much of his time was spent waiting. He was due to meet a guy who he had previously become acquainted with while doing some work on the previous two Sugar Ray fights (the not-very-exciting four-round bout against Ranzany that had probably been fixed, and the much-more-exciting one-round bout against Price that probably had not). His job today was to meet this acquaintance and finalize the plan for Sugar Ray's next fight. It was scheduled for the end of the month in Ceasers. This contact was to be a link in a chain; that would turn out to be an unnecessarily convoluted and fragile chain.

"Victor?"

Vig turned around and there he was. Ill-fitting light brown suit, open-necked shirt, and what Vig's first wife used to call 'rich-guy hair'… salt and pepper and slicked back to a curl. It was probably fashionable at the time (who remembers?) but he still looked like a douchebag.

"Hey Murray. Take a seat. I'm just about to order a drink."

Vig had hand-picked Murray for this job, partly because he was an idiot and partly because he liked to shoot his mouth off. They were not known associates of each other, and that made him perfect for what was needed. Murray's job was to bring in money from the city, and Vig's job was to get it down at the right price, and he had some people arranged to help spread it around town.

As Vig was responsible for getting the bets down, the plan was for him to spend as little time as possible with the money, and not arouse suspicion by disappearing to L.A. and suddenly placing some big action on his return. Any big bets from known sharp gamblers like Vig travelled fast through the on-strip sportbooks.

Vig finished his second drink and waited patiently for the third. As Murray prattled on it became clear that this asshole Murray could be a more of a problem than he had bargained for. The problem was that he wanted to know all the details of where the bets were being placed, who was fading the action, how much would be in cash, and whether it would be spread around. Asking too many details like this is a bad sign for a money carrier. What had happened to simply not looking in the bag? Vig sighed. Maybe he was just being paranoid. At this point he needed someone and had no real reason to think that even Murray could fuck it up.

8 SUGAR

A t the time, they called the Sugar Ray Fight the 'Benitez fight', because Benitez was getting paid twenty percent more, at least officially. There was a lot of gambling dough moving around at the time, and it would continue to be moving pretty much right up to the fight. It had been an interesting month for Vig; he had spent it walking the strip and placing bets with some of the more connected bookmakers around town. In total he had spread about five thousand dollars over eight or nine books.

Vig had a reputation to protect when it came to moving fight money and was not prepared to blow that reputation for this, so all the bets were placed in cash and all were placed in good faith. The only white lie that he told was that he was sliding in a little piece of his own money alongside the bets. The reason for all this action was obviously to move the line. Now a naked nickel won't move a line on its own, however Vig's five thousand dollars will move it like anyone else's hundred thousand. The on-strip bookmakers will assume that he is aware of some inside value and fall over themselves to move their line the other way. In fact, a sharp bettor like Vig could almost guarantee getting his action booked as sometimes the information was worth more than the potential loss, especially if the bets weren't too big. Once the line moved a few points, Vig hoped that he could get a much bigger amount down on the other side without the line moving all the way back.

So far, things were going well. The first five grand on Benitez had moved the line from plus four-eighty to almost plus four hundred. The next part of the plan was to get the bigger lump of money on Sugar Ray at the improved odds of minus four-hundred or even better. The problem was that he couldn't get this money on himself, he needed to use a third party. Someone who was not associated with him or anyone linked to the fight but could be trusted not to blow it or to steal it. Someone who did not have a reputation for making large boxing bets, and who would not arouse suspicion when they suddenly put a bundle on a fight. There weren't many people like that in Las Vegas.

Vig had arranged for a couple of guys who were coming into town to put the bets down on Sugar Ray, mixed up with some shielding action on football. They were already big-betting whales - in fact they had turned their hand at bookmaking themselves at one point - so would not arouse suspicion at some of the busier books. They weren't fronting the money of course; they were counting on Vig for the capital. He was due to hand it over - with the betting instructions - to the two whales when they arrived in from LAX just before noon. Before that he had to collect the money from Murray at the airport just before the handover. It was a tight schedule.

If this seems unduly complicated, blame Carmine.

9 CARMINE

10000 Pico Boulevard
September 15th 1979

The Hillcrest was the first Las Angeles country club to specifically cater to a Jewish clientele and sat directly opposite the original Fox movie and television studio. A lot of the already wealthy members from the movie business were enjoying the benefits of the oil crisis; the club had struck oil in the fifties and original members and their progeny were still enjoying tax-free dividends three decades later.

Vig liked operating in country clubs. They were civilized; especially compared to where he had earned most of his crusts in the past, and an invited guest was treated as well as a member. They assumed that any interlopers had 'earned' the right to be there, and his surname was sufficiently Sephardic to meet the approval of those who still checked the guestbook when an unfamiliar face was seen on the grounds.

He had built his roll by fading sports action to club members (at Hillcrest and elsewhere) by devising a unique business strategy that still is the calling card of the successful grey-market bookie today. The guys in Hillcrest were not that interested in discretion but they put a lot of value in cash.

Getting in the door was the trick – you find a member low on the pecking order and offer him amazing point spreads until he is stuck a few hundred. You then offer to write off the debt for a visit to his club and an introduction to some of the members as his 'turf accountant'. You pay out quickly, in full, and in cash. And you suddenly become the trusted guest of most of the club's members.

The club authorities tended to turn a blind eye to Vig as long as he blended in with the membership, didn't cause problems, and especially once he didn't use the pool. On this visit, Vig was lunching with Carmine E Yanuck. Yanuck was one of the last moguls of the studio system and had been forced into retirement after being ousted by his own family from his role as studio head. He sat opposite Vig now with a thin cigar clamped between his teeth, bitter as always and looking to take it out on anyone nearby.

"I can't trust my own family, Victor. So who can I trust?"

Vig's patience with him was limited. "You trust the golden rules. Don't talk about a running no-hitter. Don't bet against a team you can't name. Don't kick a dog and get surprised when he bites."

Carmine was not amused. "Leave the comedy to the circle. I'm trying to get a new studio up and running. There are two young guys – not members of the club - or the tribe for that matter - and they are providing a lot of the finance. But I don't know if they can be trusted. I'm getting old, Victor, and I might not outlive the deal… I don't really care if I don't… but it's my name. My name must outlive the deal. I want the name Yanuck to appear on a studio once again."

Vig was dubious. "Do I currently do business with these two guys?"

He laughed. "These two guys are in a similar business to you Vig. They have inheritance, and they have stocks, and have so much money, but they still want to take more of it off their friends on the baseball, basketball, football."

"They are bookies?"

"They take the Vegas lines, add their own percentage, and

book bets from their friends. Very uncivilized."

He saw the look on Vig's face.

"Not like you, Victor. You are a gentleman who runs a civilized turf accountancy for civilized people. They are strictly chai b'seret."

Civilized. Vig was starting to redefine the word. Anyway, Carmine was buying lunch, so he was in listening mode.

"I want to test them, Victor. See if they are honest. And I want you to help me."

"Carmine, this is a little unusual. How can a guy like me…?"

He silenced Vig with a wave of his hand. "Hear me out. You move money, take bets, and so on, yes?"

"Sure."

"I want to give them some information and some money, and I want to see if they try and misappropriate either."

"I don't get it."

He took the cigar from his mouth and grinned broadly.

"I know something that even you don't know. I have some information that would be very valuable to a man like you. I will share this with you on one condition, that you help me audition my two erstwhile business partners."

"How much is this information worth to me?"

"That depends on how much you are willing to bet on a sure thing. I have some information on an upcoming sporting event – a big one – that guarantees a twenty percent return, maybe more."

Vig sighed to himself. Everyone thinks they have a sure thing in sport, and maybe sometimes they do, but the problem is that if septuagenarian retirees sitting by a golf course know about it, then a hundred others do too. Everyone that gets in on a fix or a fall ends up spilling to their wife, or their brother in law, or their shoeshine boy. They cannot help themselves. That is of course, unless their livelihood depended on it. Vig decided to do what he did best; listen. Carmine duly obliged.

"How much money have you squirreled away – let's say it was forty thousand dollars? You could turn it into fifty thousand in an hour!"

An hour? That was revealing; that meant it couldn't be football, basketball, baseball, tennis or horses. He had said it was a big event, so it couldn't be anything small, which meant it could only be either hockey or boxing. This old Jew had no interest in betting on the ice-capades, so that meant that it must be boxing. If it was boxing and big, then it was Benitez vs Sugar Ray next month. The old man was still talking.

"I don't normally care about sports, but this little tidbit came to me really by accident."

Vig ignored him. He was still thinking. If it really was a twenty percent return then this meant the odds were minus four hundred, which in turn meant that Carmine must believe that he had information suggesting that Sugar Ray was a lock to win. He wondered how he had come across this information. Benitez was the underdog for sure, so a win would not be an upset. People thought the best fixes were the favorites, but the opposite was the case. A four to one underdog taking a fall did not arouse suspicion, and an insider could sell the information three times. First the result to the widest audience, then the winning round to the close associates, then the type of loss (knockout, disqualification, points, technical) to whomever he owed money to. There's a big difference in boxing between 'this is likely to happen' and 'this is a certainty'… and that was what Vig had to find out.

"Carmine, you have to understand, I often come by people who claim to have an inside track on sporting events. These people are wrong, every time, even if they get the right result. Those with real insider information don't talk, because they know that sharing devalues the information. Even if you are, by some miracle, the exception, I don't get involved in fixes. However, I also don't listen to scuttlebutt without a source."

Carmine considered this for a moment, putting the cigar back between his teeth.

"Fair enough. I see your problem. But rest assured, this is your problem. My information is good, and I intend to use it. Not to make any money, but to do a little, er…" he waved the cigar "research."

"First, I'll tell you what I would like you to do. Just ask these two big-time gamblers… these whales I guess you call them… to move money for you. I'll underwrite it, in case there's any funny business, so you don't stand to lose anything. It might be a perfect fit – if you have money you want to get on in Las Vegas, perhaps these guys could help spread it around for you."

Suddenly he was an expert on bookmakers' problems? The thing is, he was right. The biggest issue Vig had was getting bets of any size on in the legal sportsbooks in Vegas, especially on favorites.

Carmine leaned forward and spoke quietly. "If you can use these two whales to get money down for you, and they do the job straight up, that'll be all I need to know."

"You mustn't trust them that much if you want to test them?"

"I trust fucking nobody, Victor! You've always paid me on time, and for that I respect you. I know you do it to keep in business. Have you ever considered what these old studio Jews would do to you if you ever welshed on them?"

"I make it my business not to have to worry about that."

He looked at Vig thoughtfully. "I'm sure you do. Now you just need to go and figure out how much you would personally put on a sure thing."

10 AIRPORT

5757 Wayne Newton Boulevard
November 30th 1979

It was the day of the fight, and Vig was due to meet Murray at the airport to receive the eighty thousand dollars. When you spend a lot of time driving to airports without flying anywhere, parking becomes the world's biggest pain in the ass. You either valet and wait twenty minutes for your car or leave it in the parking garage yourself and walk for twenty minutes. What most people don't know is that there are places in most airports that you can leave your car without it getting towed. At this time in McCarran, it was behind the main terminal by the Flamingo check-in, about two minutes' walk from the front door. There's a place where the shuttle pulls up that's about twice as wide as it needs to be, so nobody cares if you leave your car there for a half-hour or so.

It was a simple plan: Murray would drive with the money from Phoenix in the morning and show up before twelve-thirty at the designated spot at the airport. He would park his own car in the lot and walk to where Vig was parked, then just open the door and put the bag of cash in the passenger seat beside Vig, sit in the back while it was counted, then leave. Hopefully never to be seen again.

From where Vig was parked, he could see the Pacific Southwest flight passing overhead on approach and estimated that it would take the two whales about twenty minutes from the point the plane touched down to get their baggage and leave. Vig planned on waiting exactly fifteen, then take the money around to the front door by the payphones. He knew what the two guys looked like, and they were expecting a guy with an oversized duffel bag to be standing by the entrance-hall payphones, so it seemed that everything was set.

There was a loud bang on the lid of the trunk, and Vig turned around expecting to see a shuttle driver – or maybe even airport police – looking to move him along. What he saw was Murray glancing furtively around, looking like he always did with the addition of sunglasses and an a oversized duffel bag slung over his shoulder.

Vig checked his watch then looked at Murray; it was twelve thirty-six and he sensed something was not right. Vig spent enough time around gamblers, boxers, hangers-on and hustlers, to recognize the look of the hardass vs the pussy, the baller vs the faker, and the together individual vs the individual-who-has-fucked-up.

"Open the trunk."

Vig tried to keep his voice calm. "Drop the bag in the seat and get in the back, Murray."

"Open the fucking trunk!"

Second and final chance. "Just get in."

No third chances for this guy to not be an asshole. Vig pulled the small lever to open the trunk and slowly got out of the car as Murray threw in the bag. He was babbling "I have to go. Can't stay. Er... sorry."

Vig was calm. "Just let me talk to you really quick."

"I got to go, I got someplace to be."

"Sure."

While taking the three steps towards the back of the car, Vig had scanned the surroundings to make himself certain that there was no-one in sight. By the time he'd said 'Sure' he was standing beside Murray and the open trunk. Murray tried to take a step back, but Vig grabbed him by the collar and tie and pivoted him over the tailgate until he was curled up in the trunk, and with the same motion grabbed the handle of the bag and yanked it out from under him.

For a fleeting second, the movement reminded Vig of switching the chip for the marker back on his first day in Vegas over ten years ago. He smiled at the thought. When Murray saw the smile on his lips he opened his mouth to say something, but before he could protest Vig had shut the trunk, moved around to the open driver's door, tossed the bag to the passenger side, then took the two steps back to crouch by the rear of the car.

"Don't open your mouth, or you'll get us both arrested."

"Look, I can explain…"

"Quiet. Explanations later. I've got a plane to meet."

"Yeah but…"

Vig banged the lid with the metal strap of his watch, and it had the desired effect of sounding like he had done it with a weapon. There was silence; well worth the small scratch on the paintwork.

After another quick glance to ensure he hadn't been seen, Vig moved back around to the driver's door. He took a moment to decide whether it was safer to bring it around to the valet or leave it where it was. Who could guess what the hell Murray would do? Ten seconds. Ten seconds to get the heart rate down and decide.

Vig yelled over his shoulder in the direction of the trunk as he put the key back in the ignition.

"I'm parking it out front and making the drop. Don't open your mouth, or the plan is fucked."

Within a few minutes he was calmly pulling the car up to the front of McCarran Airport. One of the valets skipped over to the car and motioned toward the trunk.

"Hey buddy, hold up. I just dropped the wife off and the silly girl forgot her medication. Can I run in and give it to her?"

"I can get one of the porters to…"

"No, she'll be mortified if anyone else does it. The meds are for her… ah." Vig pointed to his left ear.

The valet looked at him for a second, then understood.

"Just leave it here with the keys in it. If you're not back in ten, I'll park it. Deal?"

"Sounds good."

Ten minutes. Vig jumped out of the car holding two five-dollar bills and quickly handed one to his new friend. "You get the other one when I come back."

"Sure thing."

With the bag in his hand he crossed the drop-off zone to the front door and stepped into the air-conditioned lobby. The whales were both exactly where they were supposed to be, standing by the payphones. Relief. One was wearing a tan suit that appeared to be made of perfectly pressed linen (on a plane?) with a white t-shirt underneath. Beside Tan Suit stood a guy with a moustache in a sports jacket and shirt. Could have been an older cousin or brother.

Before Vig approached them, he took one more look around. There were two airport cops standing by the coffee stand and they seemed to have taken an interest, but they had no reason to be suspicious. He walked casually over to Tan Suit and Moustache. They were all business. "What exactly do we have to do with this money?"

"How about we get some lunch and I go over the details? I don't think this is the best place to have this conversation."

Tan Suit did the talking. "Hey buddy. I didn't come to Vegas to socialize with you. I'm here to have fun, watch the fight and do your boss a favor."

Vig took a deep breath.

"He is not my boss, he's a business acquaintance. I'm sure he appreciates the favor you guys are doing him, but it's my job to make sure you guys can do that favor without getting any hassle that ruins your weekend. How about I drive you to wherever you're going, and we go over the details in the car?"

They looked at each other dubiously. The cops weren't looking in their direction anymore. Vig didn't know if this was a good or bad thing.

"OK, let's eat. We have a room booked for the afternoon, let's eat there."

Afternoon? What did he mean by…?

"We're booked into the Salt Wells Villa for lunch and drinks, it's about an hour west of here."

Oh no. Of all the places…

Vig was calm, but internally he was swearing to himself. They were going to handover eighty big dimes for the purpose of betting on a fixed boxing match, and they were going to do it in a brothel just outside Pahrump.

"I know it. Let's go."

Vig headed back out to the front of the airport with the two guys holding their small weekend bags, they were practically skipping to keep up with him. When they crossed the threshold, the heat hit hard. Despite being late November, it was still noon and it was still the desert, and stepping from airport-grade air-conditioning to noon-heat was something even the locals didn't get used to. The car was still where he'd left it, which was a relief. No sign of the valet, so that was five bucks in Vig's favor.

"Keep your bags on your laps, the trunk is full."

Tan Suit moved around to the rear passenger side and got in. Moustache slid in behind him. Vig climbed in the front, put the duffel bag on the other side of the back seat, and gunned it, swinging the car across the drop off zone to the exit lane.

"Off to Fallon we go." he shouted, for the benefit of Murray. Thankfully he didn't respond, he had some sense at least. Or maybe he'd fallen asleep.

Vig already began to regret taking Murray along; it had been a spur of the moment decision that now complicated things. He had an hour to figure out what to do to ensure that the already overcomplicated plan stayed on track. He had in his car – apart from Murray - exactly eighty thousand dollars, and he had to get these two knuckleheads to bet all of it on Sugar Ray Leonard at minus four-hundred or higher to turn it into an even hundred grand.

As he drove, Vig made Moustache take a pad and pencil

from the seat pocket and write down a short list of on-property sports books who would take that action without too much risk of raising suspicion that it was part of a plot. Their job was to bet a similar amount on other events at the same time. The Sugar Ray line was close to minus-three-sixty so even these two idiots couldn't screw it up too badly. Hopefully they'd get most of the money down during the early evening, but at worst they could probably get twenty grand or so each down at Ceasers itself closer to the fight.

After Vig finished talking - and got them to tell it back to him to ensure they understood what they had to do - they began making plans for the night. No small talk. No personal talk. That suited Vig just fine; it leaked as little as possible to that shithead Murray and gave him time to figure out what he was going to say to his old friend Madam Gina Wilson once they arrived at her brothel.

11 GINA

The girl sitting across the desk from Gina raised her eyebrows "What if the customers bring something in?"

Always the same question, always the same answer. "Then make sure they bring whatever's left out with them too."

"Okay Gina, you're the boss."

The woman sitting on the other side of the small desk was close to Gina's age but looked completely different. It was the middle of the morning – before the lunchtime rush – and this was not really an interview, more of a 'welcome meeting' for the second of two girls who were starting work that day. This was not Gina's main office, this was a smaller room adjacent to the rear entrance, where the staff arrived and left for work.

"At the beginning, you can work when you want. I suggest the daytime where it is mainly regulars and a smattering of L.A. tourists. What's your working name?"

She thought for a second. "Belle, same as my real name."

A few more details and paperwork and that was it; the Salt Wells Villas had its newest employee. She had come from the 'Bottom-Up'... one of the off-strip strip clubs in Las Vegas.

Gina didn't know her personally, but she came with a recommendation from one of the regulars that she more-or-less trusted, a restauranteur from the Flamingo named Jerry. Jerry liked to come in after the lunchtime rush at his place and hang with the girls who started work at about three, before the place got busy.

Gina always watched the new girls on the first shift closely. The easiest way to do this was to simply work the bar alongside one of the regular bartenders. She could speak to the customers, get feedback, see how she got along with the other girls. In this business, money talked. If she played by the rules and made good money for herself and the house, then she could stick around. Otherwise it was a ride to the bus station.

At the Villas the girls take cash, but they'll give you a tab at the bar if you are local and Gina decides to like you. If you are a VIP with a local host's trust, then Madame might break her own rules and advance the girls out of her own roll, but the host had better pay up or they'll be cut off from not just her place, but all the other brothels in town. She might even drop the dime to the host's employer if it is one of the bigger casinos. They may thank her and fire the host, or apologize and not fire the host, but almost always they paid the tab.

This particular afternoon Jerry was in, and he had brought a buddy with him. They had both had lunch in his restaurant and had come over – beers in hand – to the bar for a drink, and to say 'hi' to Belle on her first day at her new job. Gina did not recognize the buddy; he was a lot younger than Jerry and she figured that he had just brought some acquaintance along to show off the fact that he knew a hooker personally.

When Jerry saw that Gina was working at the bar, he came over to say hello. He also took the time to pay his bar tab in full – and in cash - before ordering another pair of drinks. Gina was surprised; guys like him paid off the tab in dribs and drabs, never all at once. She opened the little grey well-thumbed book and flipped the pages until she saw the page with Jerry's name written in capital letters at the top. Gina scratched out his total, signed her name, and put the cash in the till.

It was just at that moment that Belle came out from the back with three other girls for her first line up. When customers arrived at quiet periods, the girls on duty typically came out to parade… this made it easy for inexperienced customers to settle in and not feel guilty, they could just approach the one they liked the look of. Belle seemed like a natural. She was dressed in jeans and a tight football top (she'd have to get rid of that – no sports logos on the girls as it caused arguments) and she had a bright and open smile on her face. Good for her.

Jerry didn't react straight away. For a moment, he almost looked like he didn't recognize her. When he did realize who the new girl was, he held up his beer to her in greeting, and to his delight she replied with a little wave. He didn't need any more encouragement – with a nod to his buddy he hopped off his stool and went straight over, taking her by the hand and saying hi with a smile. Off they headed to one of the backrooms. Gina guessed this was going to be a new regular for him, and that suited her fine, as long as she stayed more than a few weeks. Many girls new to the Villas – especially those new to the business – didn't last too long.

The other three girls headed back to their 'green room' and buddy stayed back in his seat by himself, while the other two patrons at the bar continued to sit and drink. They were two regulars who just came in for a beer and a view most days, saving their money till the weekend.

The tableau didn't change for a few minutes, and then Gina noticed something. Jerry's jacket was sitting on the back of the chair beside his buddy, and he seemed to be surreptitiously searching the pockets. Maybe they weren't such buddies after all.

Gina moved to the other end of the bar so that she could keep a closer eye. 'Buddy' had found what he was looking for, but she couldn't see exactly what it was. He placed whatever he had taken into his own jacket pocket, and calmly went back to his drink. He was four more beers deep by the time that Jerry returned to join him. There was no mention of whatever had been taken, Jerry just resumed his seat, and there was a brief clinking of bottles.

Gina made a show of collecting glasses near the table, and casually approached the two men. "Enjoying your afternoon?"

Jerry smiled. "All good, Gina."

Buddy didn't smile, just took a drink from his bottle. "So far." He seemed focused on a point on the opposite wall.

Another one of these type of guys; too good for a whore house, too fucking unpleasant for anyone else. Well, business was business. She'd make sure he got taken care of by one of the more experienced girls who knew how to handle these fuckers.

As she began to move away, Buddy at last opened his mouth. "Hey lady. You got a cocktail list?"

"Sure thing. Gina pulled the short list from her hip pocket and reached out to hand it to him. Before she could react, he had reached out, grabbed her wrist, and twisted her arm around and pulled her closer until they were almost nose-to-nose. He had done it quietly, so nobody else in the room had realized there was anything untoward. Gina just held his gaze for a few seconds. He must have sensed she was about to react, so he pulled her close and started to whisper menacingly in her ear.

He barely got the first word out when he heard a click below his chin. Gina didn't like guns, but that didn't stop her keeping one on her when she worked.

"Time to go."

12 SALT WELLS VILLA

Highway 50 East of Fallon
November 30th 1979

One of the girls – Vig didn't recognize which one - was outside the front dressed in her 'street' clothes having a cigarette when they got out of the car. She didn't seem surprised to see him, or maybe she had just been here long enough to know that everyone comes back again eventually.

"Hey Vig, long time no see." She looked at him quizzically. "Does Gina know you're coming?"

"Nope. Is she here?"

"Yep." She threw him a mock salute with her cigarette hand. "You picked a hell of a day. She's had an eventful afternoon. Good luck!"

The two whales carried their own bags, but Vig hung behind.

"You guys go ahead. I'll be with you in a minute."

He looked in the window of the car to check the duffel was still there – it was stuck down where he had left it in the rear driver-sided footwell. He moved around to the trunk of the car. It was likely that Murray had figured out exactly what had happened, had heard the conversation, and had decided that he was probably not getting rolled off a cliff. Vig knocked on the trunk twice, gently.

"You alive in there?"

[muffled expletives]

That was a relief. Not dead.

"We're west of Vegas, and I'm about to have lunch. I'm opening up, but if you try anything funny, I'm closing it again. Hard."

Vig opened the trunk slowly and stepped back. Murray was lying there, not looking any more crumpled than earlier. When he saw Vig he was chipper. He stepped out, tucked his shirt in, dusted himself off. It was like it never happened. "Did you get the money to the two guys?"

What a strange fucking question to ask, and it gave Vig a sinking feeling. He began to regret not counting the money.

"Before that I need you to explain something. First question: how did you get mixed up in this?"

"I don't need to answer to hoodlums like you."

"I'm not a hoodlum. I don't rob anybody. Who brought you into this job?"

"Carmine did. He vouched for me, right? That's all you wanted to know. What the hell are we doing here anyway?"

He seemed to notice his surroundings for the first time. What was he worried about? Again, Vig's mind went to the money. He hadn't opened the bag yet, was almost afraid to.

"Stay right there."

Vig moved toward him.

"What are you doing?"

"Just stay right there.

He reached into the car.

"Hold on… what are you doing?"

Vig pulled out the duffel bag. Murray flinched, presumably feeling fortunate that Vig didn't have a weapon. Then he looked again at the bag and back to Vig, and his face fell. He practically sobbed. "You mean you haven't given them the money yet?!"

"I was just about to. They're inside. So, how much are you

short?"

"You... you were supposed to give them the money at the airport."

"How much are you short?"

"It's not my fault. I... I met a bookie friend of mine I owed some money to and had to give him some of it, for a debt."

"How much are you fucking short?"

"Just twenty."

Fuck. Fucking Murray.

Well at least now Vig knew and could try and take control of the situation. The concern that had become panic, had become rage, then had eventually subsided and been replaced by focus. Time to solve this little problem, and there was no immediate benefit in taking it out on Murray's hide. This was especially not advisable in a whorehouse parking lot.

"OK. Forget lunch. Do you need to take a leak?"

"Wh... what?"

"Do you need to take a leak?"

"Why are you asking me that?"

"You're getting back in the fucking trunk."

Murray looked for a moment like he was about to protest. Vig wondered whether he would have to hit him or not. An interesting thing about shitheads like Murray is that they can take a hit to the jaw surprisingly well. Your typical mouthy street punk folds immediately. The more experienced hood can take one, but they don't tend to be so mouthy. The runners and bagmen in the boxing game could take a hit better than most, and poker players, pro-gamblers, and pimps were always able to take care of themselves to some degree. But Murray – he was the kid jogging behind the big kids, smoking the end of their cigarettes, causing trouble but never dealing with it. He'd had a lifetime of taking a hit to the jaw and getting back up. That meant that Vig didn't have to threaten anything; Murray didn't protest, he just got straight back in the trunk.

Vig headed into the Salt Wells Villas, ducking through the main entrance and turning right into the tiny diner-style restaurant. It was really just a couple of tables and a counter.

The two whales were sitting in one of the two booths with menus and what looked like a strawberry daiquiri and Coors each. They looked up as Vig approached.

"What's for lunch?"

"We always have the wings. Sit down and join us."

He slid in beside Moustache, so he could face the door and keep an eye on the car. Also, he figured that Tan Suit would do most of the talking. The waitress came over.

"You want a menu?"

"I'll have the same as these guys."

She stepped away with the order. Tan Suit spoke between slugs of his beer. "You got the money?"

"We have a small problem."

Tan Suit looked at Moustache, who appeared to mouth something to him. Tan Suit paused for a second and then looked back at Vig, seemingly resigned. "Okay, what's the problem?"

"We are a little light. The guy who was bringing the money to me at the airport was cornered by someone he owed money to, and now we are twenty thousand short."

"Goddamn it. We are just supposed to be doing you a favor… actually not even you. We're doing this for your boss."

Vig tuned out. He had had enough of this. Carmine had threatened to out the two erstwhile bookmakers to the Phoenix Country Club, which would have caused them personal and professional problems, and effectively blackmailed them into placing bets for him to ultimately act as an 'audition' for Carmine's own plans. Carmine was a tough fucker, that was for sure.

Vig waited for a few minutes for the talking to stop but it didn't, so he ended up just interrupting "You guys keep mentioning doing a favor for my 'boss'. Let's get one thing straight; I know you guys aren't doing anyone a solid; you are returning one that our mutual friend did you. I know about your little country-club gambling situation in Arizona, and Carmine" – he enunciated his name slowly to ensure it had the right impact – "made it go away, at significant personal sacrifice."

"Now wait a second…" Moustache piped up.

"No, you wait a second. We all know who we are working for, and we both know what's at stake. I've sunk five moving the line already. And now we are light another twenty thanks to Murray who got lifted because he's too stupid to keep his mouth shut when riding a cab to the airport."

"Who the crying out fuck is Murray?"

"Murray is part of the little chain that takes the money from Carmine, brings it down to Las Vegas, hands it over to me, before I hand it over to you with instructions on how to bet it."

Tan Suit. "That sounds like a lot of convoluted bullshit. I thought you used to be a money guy?"

Of course, he was right… it was a lot of convoluted bullshit. Vig certainly used to be a money guy but the problem was that everyone knew he used to be a money guy. What happens in Vegas stays in Vegas, but if Vig takes a day trip out of town and comes back and starts spreading money around on a fight, then he comes up against a lot of problems. He can't bring the money in himself. He can't place the bets himself. But he has to make sure that both of those things happen. Some people called Vig a control freak, but when you are the sole reliable person in a giant pile of fuckups then you must ensure the money gets from A to C. On top of this, his deal with Carmine was clear; hand eighty thousand in cash to Tan Suit and Moustache with instructions to bet it, then collect one hundred thousand from them the next day after they had collected the bets, then lock it in a box in the MGM to await Carmine.

Just as he had finished re-explaining the main points of this to Tan Suit and Moustache, the waitress brought his beer. Perfect timing. He took a deep hit. There was a moments silence, while the two whales contemplated their situation.

"For various reasons, we have no comeback on Murray, and I don't hold out much hope of us purloining the money back from his bookie. I've made a commitment and I'm going to honor this, and you two have made a commitment to do your part. We must get eighty thousand dollars down on Sugar Ray Leonard in the next eight hours, at minus four hundred or close to it. My job was to get the bag to you and tell you where to spread the action. I don't even know why I'm sitting here explaining this to you guys over and over, because this is now your fucking problem as much as it is mine."

"Hey man, we're not bookies. We're just golfing buddies who got a little loose booking football action at our club. We made money for Christ' sake."

Vig wanted to scream at these fuckers 'Murray stole the money because he knows Carmine would blame you for it and blow your fucking movie deal'. But of course, he didn't.

"I don't need to hear it. Eat your lunch, then we go talk to Murray and see if we can sort out this mess."

"Can't we get him to make up the difference?"

"Guys like him don't usually have twenty grand just lying around."

Moustache "Do you know where he is?"

Vig glanced toward the car park and took another hit from the bottle "Yes I do."

13 SINATRA

Circus Maximus at Ceasers
September 19th 1969

Despite the name, the Circus Maximus had little or no hint of a Roman theme. It had a pretty standard showroom motif; red oblong tables arranged in a gentle rake, small red glass candle holders, and a lot of gilt edging.

Vig was sitting alone at a table three rows from the stage, waiting for Gina, the girl who had slipped him the twenty. The table had been reserved in her name; a great seat at one of the hottest tickets in Las Vegas. Just as he began to wonder if she was really coming, she eased into the seat opposite without speaking, as if she had only come back from the powder room.

"How did you get such good seats?"

She turned to him, as if noticing him for the first time. "I have a standing reservation for all the big acts at the Circus."

Vig smiled. "You take a lot of friends here?"

She had an intriguing smile; it's funny that you don't know what that looks like until you see one. "We entertain a lot of visiting business partners, there's always someone who wants the good seats. It pays to be able to have them to hand."

Vig didn't ask what kind of business. While he hadn't been

in Vegas more than a few months, he was starting to learn a little bit about the rules that the locals follow. She detected the unasked question and cut to it herself anyway. "Do you know what kind of business I'm in?"

"If you are bringing visitors in from out-of- town rug joints like this, you must be a casino host?"

She laughed.

"No, I may work pretty closely with some of those guys, but my outfit offers a more intimate hosting service. I run one of the cathouses out west."

"Anywhere I know?"

"You been to the Salt Wells Villa out on fifty?"

"No, I have not."

This was true. He'd seen it en route to other joints in Fallon and Pahrump but was suddenly glad that he had never stopped off at that particular spot.

She continued. "That's my place. I have a string of girls – all good clean girls - in that joint, but sometimes they make it this far east to meet our most special clients and make sure they get the right exit off fifty."

"Or get off for fifty."

"Are all your jokes that terribly obvious?"

Vig smiled. "The subtle jokes that I've tried already have gone way over your head."

The curtain at the Circus Maximus stage split down the middle and the band was revealed, with boot-polish hair and brass-polish instruments. There was a burst of applause and the lights dimmed, as the conductor bowed to the audience and drew out the familiar opening notes to Bart Howard's 'Fly me to the Moon".

Gina looked like a different person in the dimmed light, with her face turned towards the music. Vig hadn't taken his gaze off her profile for a few minutes and didn't even notice that Frank Sinatra had come on stage until the crowd and the band got noticeably louder. They barely spoke another word to each other while the show went on. She seemed transfixed watching the musicians and Vig didn't want to disturb her reverie. When the first half of the show was over, the lights went up, and she snapped back into focus.

Vig - usually dead calm - almost panicked at the thought of not having something to say. "Another drink?"

"Sure. But we had better rack them up. The waiters only come near you in the second half when they want you to pay the check. Get me three bourbon old-fashioned with no ice in the glass and ask them to bring a bucket of fresh ice so I can have each one strong."

Vig asked no questions, and just beckoned over the waiter who was hovering nearby. "Six more, no ice, just an ice bucket on the side. And bring the check with the bucket."

"Yessir."

When Gina heard him ask for the check, she seemed surprised. "You closing us out already? Three drinks in forty minutes too rich for you?"

"Nope." He gave her a look.

The waiter was back quickly with the drinks. He had done as Vig had asked and left the cocktails without ice. He slid the check over to Vig, who pulled out the same twenty-dollar bill that Gina had given him at the blackjack table the last time they had spoken, making sure it was unfolded so that she could see. Written across it in dark red lipstick was the word "Labouchere".

"Keep the change." he gestured to the waiter.

"Thank you, sir."

She looked at Vig quizzically. "You still have that twenty? Maybe you are cheaper than you think."

"Tell me what you meant by it. I know some people call the Labouchere the 'split'. Maybe you were giving me a hint of your system, in the hope I'd deal the streaks just right to make you a winner. Or maybe you were advising me to get out of there?"

She appeared to consider this for a moment before responding. "Labouchere was an English aristocrat. Rich, powerful, but he always made time to gamble. Married some homely actress."

"Were you suggesting I find myself a homely actress?"

"Maybe you should keep better company than the dealers at an unlicensed Red Rock blackjack table."

Vig smiled "Do you think fifth-row seats opposite a cathouse madam is a step up?"

The moment he said it, he wondered was it a step too far. She paused for a second, then broke into a laugh. A deep laugh, that made the people at the tables next to them turn their heads.

The drinks arrived, exactly how Vig had ordered them.

She unceremoniously tossed the ice tongs aside and reached into the bucket with her hand and grabbed a handful of fresh ice. She dropped two cubes each in two glasses, dropped the rest of the ice back in the bucket, and pushed one of the glasses over to Vig.

"So, what did she tell you? That I was going to be martingaling?"

"That quite a fucking non-sequitur."

"Well?"

"Yes, she told me you like to Martingale. You were supposed to be a degenerate doubler?"

"And you or one of the other dealers were there to make sure I lost four grand this time around."

He paused. "How do you know this?"

"Beryl Cameron-Gibbons, or whatever she's called back in England, has a bone to pick with you."

Vig took a hit from the old fashioned. Strong. Maybe there was something in this separate-ice deal. "I'm sure she did after I walked out on her job."

"No, before that. She was setting you up."

At that moment, the lights dimmed, and the rear curtains began to slowly part again, to reveal the band in place, and Frank sitting in the center of the stage on a stool, holding an identical glass to the one Vig was holding.

Gina leaned over. "Don't get mad. I was… kind of in on it."

14 CALICO

San Diego
Early 1950s

When Gina told Vig that she was in on it he was shocked. As far as he knew, Beryl Cameron-Gibbons did not have any reason to bear a grudge, despite them having more than a little history.

His first encounter with Miss C-G was memorable. Vig had been tasked with delivering some money to her at a small local fight in San Diego. They hadn't met before, but everyone knew the one-of-a-kind 'British blonde bombshell of boxing'. The delivery was due to take place at an off-books fight happening at a small local club. These fights were sometimes run as rematches for officially retired fighters or for newly professional boxers to get some competitive fights under their belt without hurting their statistics or reputation.

One of the bouts on the undercard was a rematch between a retired fighter named Calico, and the opponent he had lost to in his final pro bout. Calico maintained that at the end of that fight the bell had been rung early when he had his opponent on the ropes, blaming everyone from his own manager, his opponent, the venue, his own family, and the boxing fraternity… accusing them all of keeping him from a final professional win to round out his career. Vig knew Calico well and was interested in seeing if he really was able to reverse the previous result and get the win that he felt he deserved.

Calico's bout was listed as third-last, and Vig arrived at the small boxing club early in the undercard when the place was already three-quarters full. Just after taking his seat he got a tap on the shoulder from another boxer who he recognized but who was not on the card. Apparently, Calico wanted Vig to wish him luck in person in the dressing room. Vig wondered if he wanted him to fade a bet on Calico's own bout or take some action on other fights on the card? There was only one way to find out.

So back he went, led by the boxer through the crowd and towards the doorway leading to what passed for locker rooms at this small club. Calico was there, dressed in his shorts, shirtless and shoeless, with partly wrapped fists. The moment he saw Vig, he went on an expletive-heavy tirade, berating him for showing up to the fight.

"This place ain't safe, Vig. It ain't safe. Why'd you have to come here? It's going to get boosted Vig, the whole room is going to get boosted."

This is not what Vig expected to hear. Vig could barely make any sense out of him. It took him a full minute to understand what he meant. Not only was Calico planning to beat his opponent fair and square and bet heavily on himself, he was also planning to have some of his friends' friends rob the place afterward to exact some sort of revenge on the boxing community.

They had first become acquainted during the latter part of his career, so he Calico figured that Vig was worth keeping out of trouble. Vig thought it was possible that the boxer was bullshitting for some reason, maybe he was planning on taking a fall and didn't want any knowing eyes on it. Vig told him as much and told him that his plans wouldn't change, that he was sticking around. Calico didn't want to listen.

Vig couldn't just make the delivery and leave, as this would arouse even more suspicion if the place was robbed.

Thankfully Vig had already decided to keep the cash loose in his glove box and instead carry an empty bag with him to the fight, a simple security ploy he would adopt for much of his money-moving career.

As it turned out, the planned robbery never happened. Vig found out later that the team Calico had been in cahoots with had seen the size and demeanor of the crowd at the club and bailed out, believing it was too risky. However, by sheer coincidence a completely different set of out-of-town hoods showed up to rob the place during the middle of the card.

They did a professional job, targeting only the cash, bags and watches, and generally sticking to the front few rows at the event where the wealthier patrons would be found. They moved methodically down each row working in pairs; one held the bag and the gun, and the other shook down each patron in turn.

Once they had finished the first two rows, one pair of hoods broke off the pattern and came straight to Vig. He guessed it was some sort of setup or tipoff that he would be there and holding cash. Vig handed over the empty bag with a smile. He wasn't worried; they were a professional crew so wouldn't waste any time looking at the contents, unless they had also been tipped off that extracting other people's money from Victor Green wasn't so easy.

The team left as quickly as they arrived; the two pairs leaving first, quickly followed by their confederates who had been guarding the doors, and then presumably one or two lookouts that were no doubt posted outside.

The cops came and went. A handful of statements were taken from the people who were prepared to talk to them. The bizarre thing was, almost everyone stayed. Nowadays this would have caused pandemonium, multiple calls to the cops, calls to their lawyers, but this crowd came to see the fights and they wanted the fights to continue. The cops agreed to leave a couple of guys posted outside while they went through the rest of the card. Only in San Diego.

Once the hubbub had died down and the bouts had

resumed, Vig was able to discreetly slip out and retrieve the real bag of cash from his car, and get it to Miss C-G, exactly as he was contracted to do. When he returned with the bag Miss C-G was not amused. "What do you think you are doing? Did you know this place was going to get turned over?"

Vig laughed "That's the first time I've ever had a complaint from someone who got paid."

She grabbed the bag and pushed it under her chair while looking around furtively. "You keep your mouth shut about this. If anyone asks, you paid me before the robbery."

Paying her early would have put the heat on him as his contract was clear in relation to when she should be paid, and under what circumstances, and Vig had stuck to the terms to the letter. He told her as much "No-can-do Miss C-G. That's not how this works. I'll tell the sender exactly what happened. The minute I get a rep as a liar, then that's the end of my rep."

She was a little put out by this but in the end had accepted it and grudgingly thanked him for saving her roll. From that point on it seemed to Vig that things were a little cooler between them. Probably for the best. In the end, she was proven right. She took some flak for being the only one to carry any cash out of the robbery. While Calico's buddies had been frightened off by the local hoods and told to stay away, Calico himself took a lot of heat for the rumors surrounding his involvement. A total clusterfuck of a night, and of a fight, and what should have been a feather in Vig's cap and a boost to his reputation, turned out to be something he tried hard to forget.

Since this incident, Vig hadn't held money for her again as far as he knew. Vig was glad; she was a tough cookie and had a reputation for paying those who crossed her back in kind.

15 GALAXIE

3595 Las Vegas Boulevard South
September 19th 1969

The Desert Villa was built in the mid-1950s, and after a few years Phil Empey decided to add his surname to the sign. It boasted seventy-two air-conditioned rooms, with a TV in each. It was notable as a family friendly joint with a pool out front, visible from the road. When it was built it stood right on what would become one of the 'four corners' on the strip. It also served - right up until it became the Cromwell - a great breakfast from 2am to noon, and that's why Gina and Vig were often found there.

On this particular morning they sat opposite each other in a narrow booth. There were about two dozen other tables in the low-lit room, and most of them were full. Waitresses moved from table to table with iced water, french toast, fresh orange juice, scrambled eggs, pots of fresh coffee, and of course the obligatory Bloody Mary.

Normally when you are eating breakfast just before dawn like this, you can split the crowd into two groups; those that are about to start the day early and those about to finish the day late. However, it was much more difficult to split the crowd in this joint. Half of them were coming in from a night on the tiles, half of them were up early for a drive to the Hoover Dam or the canyon or to catch a flight, and the rest could have been at a business lunch. Not drunk, not disheveled, just getting outside their eggs like it was eight-thirty a.m. in the city and they were heading off to Wall Street.

"So, when she went back to her bar in England, the rumors surrounding the robbery followed her. Her own bar – the Thomas-A-Beckett – had also been turned over in suspicious circumstances while she was away, so the authorities had put two plus two together. That's apparently why she took early retirement in Vegas."

"How do you know all this?"

"You remember the two customers that my staff were escorting that night. They were pillow-talkers."

"And she blamed me?"

"Not entirely. She thought you were a small cog, and when you refused to do her bidding, she filed that away under 'fuck this guy' or whatever. There were a few other scores settled that night, if you recall, and one or two others planned to be scored, if you recall." She wiggled her eyebrows suggestively.

After her admission, Gina ate opposite Vig in silence, focusing on enjoying her French toast. She picked it apart with her fingers, dipped it in the little metal bowl of maple syrup, and savored each piece, taking her time. When the last piece was done, and the last drop of syrup mopped up, she sat back in her chair and looked him dead in the eyes.

"Are you sober enough to drive?"

"I don't have my car."

"My car is parked in the Flamingo next door. Let's go for a spin."

There was no arguing with her. It was a warm morning, although the sun hadn't quite risen yet. There was something beautiful about the strip at this hour; the streets were quiet, with just a few revelers of the night making their way home. It was strange; despite the relatively peaceful streets Vig knew that there were still fortunes being made and lost all over town, and marriage vows being made and broken.

It was a couple of minutes' walk around the side of the hotel to the entrance to the guest parking garage at the back of the Flamingo hotel. The valet desk was unmanned.

"They'll have probably left the keys under the wheel."

They walked straight past the desk towards the parking garage and found her car. It was a red Ford Galaxie two-door convertible that looked almost new. She reached down under the front wheel and smiled.

"Bingo."

The V8 engine roared and the custom whitewall tires squealed as they pulled out of the parking garage onto East Flamingo Road and turned southbound down the strip. Vig had no idea where they were headed, and he didn't give a shit.

16 GINA

Highway 50 East of Fallon
November 30th 1979

The wings were good. It was somehow reassuring to Vig that Gina's place still did good food. He asked the waitress to wrap up a sandwich for him, picked up the check, then gestured to Tan Suit and Moustache.

"Come with me out to the car."

They headed back out to the parking lot. Vig walked over to the car and reached down to the trunk handle.

"Now don't make a big deal about this."

He pulled open the trunk. Murray was lying there with his hands crossed over his chest, like he had been asleep. He still seemed relaxed, almost serene.

"I hope you got me some take out. Or maybe cigarettes?"

The two whales looked at each other, then at Vig. Vig reached into his pocket and pulled out the sandwich, which he tossed at Murray in the trunk.

"Guys, this is Murray. This is the guy who has ripped us – and more importantly our mutual business associate – off."

"I didn't rip you off Vig. I just got unlucky." He looked at the three figures standing over him in turn. "Can one of you guys give me a ride back to town?"

Vig almost admired Murray's bravado. "We're not done with you. You are going to help us make the stake whole, or you and I are driving this car back to L.A. so you can explain yourself."

"I can get the twenty g's. I have people I can rely on."

"Twenty grand in" – Vig looked at his watch – "three hours. I doubt it. I am pretty sure the line won't move until maybe six-thirty, after that there'll be other money going on the fight and fucking up the line we were paid to bet."

"I got a guy who'll lend us the money."

"What do you two think?"

Tan Suit spoke. "We've got plans in there" – he pointed back at the cathouse we had just come from – "for the next couple of hours, then we head back into Vegas. We've a car picking us up here at three and driving us around town to spread a little money around before we go ringside."

Vig bit his lip. "We'll have the money to you by four o'clock."

Tan Suit seemed doubtful. "Not a minute later."

The two figures turned and walked back towards the front door of the Villas.

Vig was about to reply, but he was cut off by a female voice from behind him. A voice he hadn't heard in years, but one that he could never forget.

"Hey stranger. You think a thirty percent tip makes up for not saying hello?"

"Hey lady, this is a private conversation."

Murray was standing there with a half-unwrapped sandwich. Vig lost whatever remaining patience he had had with Murray. "Shut up and get in the car. I'll be there in a minute."

Vig turned back towards the voice. "Good to see you Gina."

She had stepped out from the main entrance, passing the two whales as they headed back in. She was dressed casually, but she still looked the very same as the last time Vig had seen her almost five years previously.

"Vig. I told you to keep your bullshit away from me, and away from this place. Take your luggage" – she pointed towards Murray – "and get out of here."

"I really didn't mean to end up out here. I business with two of your customers, and they insisted on coming along for the ride. Turned out that they liked the food as much as I used to."

She couldn't hide a brief smile, but it disappeared fast. "Just go, Victor."

"You know we have some unfinished business" He looked behind him "But this is not the time."

A flash of sadness seemed to briefly pass her face. "There's nothing you need to say to me, Vig."

Vig heard a noise and turned around. Murray was leaning over from the rear seat of the car and honking the horn. Gina cocked her head sideways. "You look like you're in some kind of trouble Vig."

"That remains to be seen. How do you know Murray?"

She laughed and pointed up at the red and white sign announcing 'Salt Wells' with the image of the three girls dancing below it. "I know everybody."

Of course, Murray had overheard. "Come on Gina. I thought your place was supposed to be discreet?"

She shouted directly at Murray. "My level of discretion is inversely proportion to the size and tardiness of your tab."

She lowered her voice. "What are you mixed up in?"

She seemed genuinely concerned, but Vig knew better than to get her involved with something like this, even if she could help. He decided to be straight with her.

"There's a fight tonight. I'm committed to get a bet down on it for a client. We are short a little money."

She smiled. Vig began to reconsider… after all, she did know the secrets of a lot of people in town. Certainly, a lot of the men. "Shall we go for a spin?"

And that was that – all was forgiven. At least for the moment.

17 CHUCK

5410 Paradise Road
November 30th 1979

They had stopped at Vig's motel to get Murray a
shower and a shave. When he was ready, they
headed out to the Other Place, a small bar on
Paradise Road near the back of the Tropicana.

The Other Place was known as a pretty hot joint every
night, but during the day the back room was unofficially sub-
let to an illegal bookmaker named Chuck, who Vig had heard
of but didn't know personally. Today had been a day of
mistakes, so he figured that another few fuckups wouldn't
make much difference.

Gina was typical Gina. Her approach to life seemed to be
to collect unfinished business, and she and Vig had plenty. She
had ridden with them back to Vegas, while Murray sat in the
back, objecting to almost every part of the plan that they
concocted en route.

"Why Chuck?" he kept asking.

Gina's response seemed simple. "Chuck will give you – or
rather us – credit, so you can fill that hole in Vig's bankroll and
get your bet down."

Vig was worried about this part of the plan; he hadn't been

83

aware that she had known any bookies that well, and certainly didn't think she knew any who would give her twenty thousand dollars' worth of credit. However, she was not stupid and Vig trusted her when it came to this sort of stuff, despite the years that had passed. Even more importantly, he had no other options.

"We're here to see Chuck."

Gina knocked on the shutters in front of the Other Place. They had parked right outside. Vig wanted to leave the money in the car – out of habit - but Gina insisted they take it with them.

A small window opened behind the shutters, and a gruff voice replied. "We are closed."

Gina replied "We know. We are here to see Chuck."

"Chuck is not expecting any visitors."

Vig spoke up. "I have some information about an imminent sporting event that he might be interested in."

A face came close to the shutters. "Chuck's not interested."

Before he had a chance to tell them to fuck off, Gina interjected "Tell him the information is from Victor Green."

Vig gave her a look. She gave him a look right back. The face disappeared for a moment. A moment later they heard a bolt being thrown, and then the noise of the shutters being wound up from inside. The owner of the disembodied voice was a surprisingly short, squat, man wearing a three-piece suit and a pince-nez. He was dressed like a middle-aged man, but only looked in his late thirties or early forties. He poked his head out the door, and looked at Murray, then Gina, then Vig.

"Victor I assume. I don't believe I've had the pleasure."

Gina looked over at Vig. "I told you your reputation would precede you!"

Chuck turned to Gina. "And you are?"

"Gina Wilson. We've met before."

"I'm afraid I don't know the name."

A puzzled look came over her face. "I own the Salt Wells Villa out on fifty."

He looked blankly at her for a moment. It wasn't clear if he recognized who she was and wanted to conceal it, or just didn't care. "Victor. Miss Wilson. Come inside. The man who I choose to refer to as your driver stays outside."

Murray continued to not know when to shut up. "What the hell do you…"

"Murray, just relax. You don't have to go back in the trunk."

"Can I at least turn on the air and the radio?"

"Sure." Vig tossed the keys to him. "Just don't touch anything else."

Gina stepped inside, and Vig followed her in. The place was dark, but surprisingly airy inside. You expect a bar at this end of town to be a dive, but this place had a certain opulence about it. There was a large mirror down the right wall, with a wide wooden bar with about a dozen leather stools tucked under it. The ceiling had two large, modern, chandeliers hanging directly above the bar, and there were a few other smaller tables on the opposite wall. The lack of seating in the middle of the room suggested that this was a place that was accustomed to dancing.

There was a stack of papers on the bar, and a small tumbler with a few pens and pencils in it. A large silver coffee pot stood beside the stack of papers. This must have been where Chuck had been sitting when they knocked on the door. Sure enough, he climbed back onto the stool and beckoned for his two guests to sit beside him.

"You will have some coffee?"

"Sure." They both spoke at the same time.

He walked around behind the bar and got three small plain glass cups from a shelf directly adjacent to where he was sitting and placed them on the bar. There were no handles on the cups, and no saucers or spoons were produced. He was in no hurry. As he prepared the coffee, he spoke softly.

"I presume this is something to do with the undercard tonight?"

Without waiting for an answer, he half-filled the three cups of coffee. When he was done, he walked back around the bar towards his seat.

"There's a lot of people in town, and I've already booked a lot of action. My ledger is fairly balanced at this stage, not that I would be taking a penny of your action anyway."

"So why did you let us in?"

"You clearly want something from me, and you claim to have something to offer me. I presume it's not early news about a basketball player with a sprained ankle." He chuckled to himself. "So, just tell me what you want, and give me a hint as to what you have, and let's see if the two are worth a trade."

"You say your book is balanced on all the fights tonight?"

"Pretty much."

"If I needed to get some money on a fighter, could you get the bet on for us?"

He took off his pince-nez and began cleaning it. "I can't book any of your action I'm afraid."

"No, I mean get the bet on elsewhere?"

"Why can't you place the bet yourself... or get one of your friends to do it?"

This was the delicate part. Smart bookies like Chuck made money by taking money up front. It was not their style to give credit. They left that to the gangsters, who would happily give credit to losing bettors, so they'd keep the juice on the bet and the interest on the credit.

Vig took a deep breath. "We have eighty in cash. I need to get one hundred on a certain fighter, at a certain price."

He narrowed his eyes but kept cleaning his glasses. "That's two big numbers. That's two very different numbers. I'm not hearing any good reason for extending you twenty thousand dollars in credit."

There was no point in beating around the bush with this guy. "I have information on the Benitez fight and was hoping that would change your mind."

His hands stopped.

"One of them is taking a dive?"

"You can get the bet on for us, with your own line of credit. Or you can pay us the twenty grand in cash for the information, if you don't act on it until maybe an hour before the fight."

He looked skeptical. He was probably trying hard to look skeptical. "Exactly how did you come by this information?"

"I'm putting a lot of someone's money on the fight. I guess it stands to reason that it is somebody who knows something more than the oddsmakers."

This was true, but in every way misleading.

"You've been involved in fixes before?"

"I don't fix fights."

He smiled sarcastically. "Of course, you don't. You are the famous Victor Green; you just carry bags. You don't know what is in them, or who it is for, or who it is from. You are always innocent. So, what am I supposed to do with this information? The local line has been lengthening all month, lot of smart money doesn't think Sugar Ray has it in him."

It was Vig's turn to smile. He had to show that his information was good, without tipping his hand. "The person putting the big slug down has already put five – through me – around town. The reason you haven't already seen me is that I don't bet off-strip."

Chuck was aghast. The polite exterior dropped, and the face and voice of a dog-track bagman appeared.

"You're shorting the fucking whole line on a fixed fight? They may be rug joints, but if these assholes find out you are bending them over with fix money then they won't just call gaming on you. There's plenty of advantage players and shorters turning up under dirt for way less than a nickel."

"I'm placing bets. The strip books are aware of my reputation and are adjusting their line accordingly. I'm not playing Chinese whispers, I put the money down like anyone else."

"I'd like to know a little more about your, ah…" he gestured to the bag "… boss."

Vig sighed. There was no going back now.

"There is mostly no boss. This is mostly my own cash."

Vig let let that sink in.

"Two-thirds mine, the rest owned by someone who you've heard of but never met." He hoped the theatrics would dissuade further questions.

Gina looked at Vig, eyes wide. "What about all that bullshit about Murray?"

"That wasn't bullshit. I had a friend send the money down here via Murray. He was chosen because he has a big mouth, so that nobody would wonder why I'd kept my roll off the line."

"And the two whales?" she was incredulous. He hated lying to her, but he didn't think it was wise to share all the details, yet.

"I'm doing someone a favor by getting this money down via these guys, and that someone is pretty certain that barring a heart attack, Leonard is winning this fight."

Chuck looked from Vig, to Gina, and back again. "Is he telling the truth?"

She shrugged... looked at Vig and nodded. "He's unlikely to lie about this stuff. He's one hundred percent never going to lie to me. He's also fronting a fair bit of cash. I say no, he's not lying."

Chuck appeared to consider this for a few seconds.

"OK. I'll take the eighty in cash now and spot you the twenty."

He laughed. Just like that.

"Truth is; I can get this on with another bookie I know that has been beating the line on Benitez all week. Sugar Ray has been slacking off at camp, so this bookie figures with the market moving like that, that he was taking a dive."

"That was the idea."

"Do you happen to know what round he is going down in?"

"He's going to go as far as he can. He'll be on his back early in the fight to keep the points gap, but it will be a scrap. He's throwing a title away, but he's making over a million dollars to buy more farmland, and then going to move up in weight again. He started out fighting light and still thinks he's light, so he's packing it on to take on Hope."

Chuck shook his head. "These crazy fucking Puerto Ricans – they think they can take on everyone."

"This Benitez guy can. He's going to hurt Sugar Ray, that's for sure. But no KO."

Chuck paused and leaned back on his stool.

"If I get this money down with another bookie, and he finds out it came from someone close to the fight, then I end up with a whole heap of problems, the least of which would be a distinct downturn in business. Some of my clients are... intolerant of shenanigans. I will be able to get this on at minus three eighty, and it'll take me a few days to collect. That'll be one hundred and thirty thousand dollars for you this time next week. If Benitez fucks up and wins, you'll have to pay me back the twenty, plus another twenty on top."

"Why another twenty?"

"Because fuck you that's why." The smile never left his face. He pointed at Gina with one hand and Vig with the other. "And you'll both be on the hook for it."

Vig tried to object, but she put her hand on his shoulder "It's alright Vig. I trust you."

Considering their history, he was surprised to hear her say that.

Vig remembered something. "One small thing, Chuck. I won't be collecting the bets myself; they will be collected by a guy in a tan suit and a guy with a moustache."

He looked at Vig and nodded. "Tan suit and a moustache. If anyone else shows up with that description, you are out of luck, you understand?'

"I understand."

Gina lifted the bag of cash onto the bar and pushed it across the bar. Chuck didn't even look at it. Why would he? If they shorted him, he could have voided the deal and kept the money.

Chuck returned his attention to his paperwork, and it was time for them to leave.

They stepped out into the daylight and turned down towards where the car was parked. It was not the first time that Vig had handed over his entire net worth – and a little bit of someone else's - to someone he'd just met, but somehow, he was not worried about that, he was worried about how he had roped Gina into it.

She noticed before he did. "Shit."

The car – and Murray – were gone.

She yelled back towards the open door of the bar. "Hey Chuck, can you call us a cab?"

A short cab ride later and they were pulling up outside the Sands; the two whales were standing exactly where they said they would be. Gina and Vig didn't really need these two anymore, but as he hadn't really held up his end of the bargain with Carmine, Vig was going to try and recover the situation as much as he could.

As they climbed out of the rear of the cab, Tan Suit looked dubiously from Vig to Gina. "Where's the money?"

"Change of plan. You guys are off the hook. We got the money down elsewhere. You guys just have to collect."

This did not elicit the relief or joy that Vig had expected. The two of them stepped forward and the taller one spoke. "Off the hook? Does that mean we're clear with…?"

"Yep. Clear." Vig could feel Gina's eyes burrowing into the back of his head.

The two whales shared a glance. It was the smaller one's turn to speak. "We've got a car bringing us to Caesars for the fight. We've got a couple of extra tickets; you should join us."

"Where?"

"Fifty feet from the sweat."

Vig had to admit, the idea did appeal.

He had not intended going to the fight, as he didn't want to be spotted speaking to these two guys; who knew who they had been talking to? But now there was no reason to turn it down, and a big fight was a big fight. However, Vig could tell that Gina wasn't so sure. Before he had time to reassure her, a car pulled to a stop behind them right where their cab had been. They turned around; it was a white Cadillac Fleetwood limousine – typical – and the driver had smartly stepped out to open the rear passenger door. Vig knew a lot of local limo drivers, and this was not one that he recognized, but he wasn't looking for reasons to worry.

"After you, Miss." Tan Suit was standing by the driver, beckoning them to get in.

This seemed too easy, the whales weren't even curious as to what had happened to Murray, or the missing money. Vig should have listened to his gut.

18 SUGAR RAY

Caesars Palace Sports Pavilion
November 30th 1979

From the ABC TV broadcast:

*[Sugar Ray Leonard, leaving his dressing room, ready to walk through this packed
Arena and come on into the ring. Twenty-three years of age. Height: five-ten. Weight: one-
forty-six. Twenty-five victories, sixteen of them by knockout. Those are the simple statistics
on this kid. What they don't state is what has happened with him and the American public.
A growing love affair. Because he seems so clean, and is so clean, and has so much
personality.]*

This was not like the Vegas stadiums of today – it was
smaller, louder, and drunker. They had built the
Pavilion almost as an afterthought, out past the
hotel pool, and it looked like nothing more than an airplane
hangar from the outside. Inside wasn't a lot more impressive,
with bleachers on all four sides beyond the temporary floor
seats. The reason fights were staged here were simple; the place
was lousy with those larger klieg lights that made the place look
a lot better on a twelve-inch black and white TV set.

The almost-capacity crowd rose to their feet as the two
boxers approached the center of the canvas.

[*That smile flashes. There are similarities of course to other fighters of the past. His manager will tell you that he uppercuts in the manner of Basilio, his lateral movement is in the manner of Dupas, the jab operates like Pastrano's. But then there are those who have begun to say that he could become another Sugar Ray Robinson.*]

Las Vegas was the home of top-level boxing, and there was nothing like a Las Vegas fight. The atmosphere was unique because the mix of attendees was unique. Attending the big fights had become a status symbol for the West Coast elite; the closer to the sweat, the bigger deal you could claim to be. Among them mixed the upper echelons of the boxing community from both coasts. The rest of the crowd was made up of a heady mix of comped tourists, boxing fans, gamblers, and a massive cohort of Puerto Ricans who had come to watch Benitez get another title to match the two he had already won and defended.

[*Back, live, in Las Vegas! The tale of the tape: Leonard at twenty-three. Rafael Benitez only twenty-one. Sugar Ray Leonard hasn't faced the caliber of opponent that Rafael Benitez has. But with his most recent fights - especially when he KO'd Andy Price in the very first round, a man who had beaten Cuevas and Palomino - he has started gaining respect.*]

Vig sat about fifteen yards from ringside, with Tan Suit on his left at the end of the row, and Gina on his right with Moustache sitting right beside her. He couldn't shake the feeling that they were penned in. Directly in front of this happy foursome were four empty seats. No doubt someone was cutting it fine, or more likely still busy with dice or girls.

[*In Sugar Ray Leonard's corner; Dundee, Dave Jacobs, James Spartan. And in Benitez's corner, Argentario Benitez. The father who said in a recent magazine piece that he wouldn't sit in his son's corner for two hundred thousand dollars. Criticized his son for not training. I'll tell you; Benitez has sure trained for this one. He has never been in such superb condition.*]

The crowd was still on its feet when the bell rang, and at the same moment a group of four sharply dressed men filed in to fill the seats in front of them. The first of them was older, with a grey suit and glasses, and the other three looked like they all went to the same tailor, with dark blue three-piece suits that could have been new, but also would have been the height of fashion about fifteen years beforehand.

[A minute left to go in the round! Benitez and Leonard. First evidence there of Benitez counterpunching. Leonard apparently with the stronger punch. Ringside experts agree on that.]

The party of four in front were not particularly animated during the first round, but they did seem to be intently focused on the action. The two on the left occasionally turned their heads to speak quietly to each other. As the bell rang, Grey-Suit-Glasses suddenly turned around to Tan Suit and spoke. "Our friend here was wondering if you would like to switch seats with him, for a better view of the action?"

Tan Suit almost jumped out of his skin. "Er... no thanks guys. I'm all set here."

The third man in front – the most heavy-set of the three – stood up suddenly but did not turn around and spoke quietly. "Buddy. Get the fuck up and let Mr. Sacco sit down". Vig felt Gina grip his hand tightly. He decided to try and put her at ease.

"Go ahead and switch. I guess Ronald wants to have a chat with me."

Vig didn't know what would happen when he called Sacco by his first name. Grey-Suit-Glasses just smiled, the other three didn't seem to react. Moustache stood up and took the empty chair, and the heavy-set Ronald Sacco slid around and sat down beside Vig, without even taking his glance away from the ring.

[Benitez, out of action the past seven months. Some figure that may have hurt him. The end of the round at hand.]

"Been a while Victor."

"I didn't realize I'd been missed, Ronald."

"Oh yes, I know you've been around. I heard you'd broken the habit of a lifetime and were betting your own money on Benitez. Those goddamn top-line bookies are so scared of your lousy five that they moved their line. If I didn't know better, I'd say you were working this fight, but I know you don't usually watch fights that you work, do you?"

Vig said nothing.

[Round two just getting underway. You should have heard Dundee talking to Sugar Ray Leonard in the corner between rounds. "Don't let that bum stare you down! Let him have it back! You'll stiffen him! You'll stiffen him with the left hook off the jab!" But that is Dundee talking, Leonard's manager. A different story in the other corner, of course.]

"The boy looks like he wants it. Is your friend Sugar-Ray going to take a dive?"

Vig turned towards him. "I don't have any friends in this fight. You know I've placed bets for plenty of people in the past."

"I need to know who has fixed this fight."

"I have no idea what you are talking about. Anyway, we're almost three rounds in, what does it matter? You hoping to get a bet down?"

[...when you have Benitez against the ropes, that's the time to be wary. That's what happened to Palomino...]

He leaned forward. "I need to know who has fixed this fight. I have my reasons."

[...a slip by Benitez!]

"I bet you do. However, I'm afraid that I don't have the information that you want. I just move money for other people. I don't get involved in fixes, I don't get involved in doping, and I don't get involved in ringers. But you know all that already. You also know I don't get leaned on."

[Remember, the left Jab is the key from Leonard's point of View. Leonard's hand and foot speed is at times dazzling. Benitez, beginning to throw his own left in this round.]

"You don't get leaned on? That just means you haven't been leaned on by someone who is serious about it. In any case Victor, I'm not leaning on anyone. A fixed fight is a fixed fight whether you are in on it or not, and if you are betting thousands of dollars of your own money then you know more than most. I want to know what you know, and how you know it."

[Fourth round underway. One knockdown in the third. A quick, short left by Sugar Ray Leonard, flooring Benitez! Embarrassing him. He tried to laugh and sneer it off.]

Vig kept his tone level and avoided turning his head.

"You've clearly done your research on me. Let me guess what you learned. Victor Green; small time specialist bookie, occasional west coast small time money runner, occasional sharp bettor. Can be trusted to move money without getting distracted, sticky, or unnecessarily robbed. Shuts the fuck up about his work at every opportunity."

[But when he got back to his corner, there was blood coming from the mouth. So now the champion knows that Leonard is for real! There's an intense concentration about Leonard in this fight.]

Sacco grunted. "You forgot 'Associates with a whore'."

[He has taken to posturing within the ring. He had become kind of brash with his statements a la Ali, but not before this fight. A change of attitude. Fourth-round action. Again, that quick left of Leonard's getting in there.]

Vig could feel Gina stiffen beside him, but he smiled. A guy who resorted to insults so quickly was desperate. Now he was sure that Sacco had no fucking idea whether Vig knew anything or not. These hoods could be so dumb sometimes.

[Leonard, with quicker hands getting the better of the exchange.]

"Sacco. If we are going to sit here and throw words around, I could throw around a few of my own."

[Leonard left in the fourth round! A caution from Padilla, a rightful caution, because Ray had half swung at Benitez's body. This fight, and the anticipation that surrounded it, brings it back to the old days of boxing, as the two go at it, with a brisk exchange.]

In Vegas, all you need is a moment of luck. Vig and Gina got theirs in the shape of an old friend of Vig's called Jeorg. Vig hadn't seen him in over a year, and right now he was standing in front of him.

Jeorg grinned broadly and practically yelled. "Hey Vig, what are you doing here? Are you working?"

The heavies both looked at Vig. The taller one barked at Joerg to move along, in a tone that sounded like it was used to being obeyed quickly; he hadn't contended with someone like Jeorg.

Joerg was unflappable. Joerg was crazy. Joerg happened to be six foot two and be in the same shape he was in when he left the army in his early twenties. Joerg also gave no fucks.

"Hey, I'm just saying hi to my friend!"

[The Bell has just sounded for round five.]

Vig didn't want to get his friend in trouble. He kept any anxiousness out of his voice. "Good to see you Joerg. Maybe we'll get a drink after the fight."

In the meantime, the taller heavy had had enough. "Buzz off, you Kraut fuck."

Vig looked at Gina, who looked back at him, bewildered. This might be a chance. The heavy-set guy stood up quickly, but before he could even begin to remonstrate with the tall

European, things escalated. Jeorg immediately dropped the drink he was carrying and laid out heavy-set with a single punch high on his chest, almost at his neck. Heavy-Set was on the ground gasping before they knew what had happened.

[*The right nostril of Benitez was worked on between rounds. Blood from it. It had been bloodied a couple of weeks ago while in training by a sparring partner and may have been rendered vulnerable. Leonard's left has been working effectively. Fans in the arena who are from Puerto Rico are all rooting and chanting for Benitez.*]

Vig thought fast. Heavy-Set was down. He figured the two whales and Sacco would stay where they were, so they just needed to get away from Grey-Suit-Glasses. "Thanks, Joerg. We need a twenty second head-start."

[*Still fighting with caution. Leonard goes down to the belly or tries to. And Leonard can't. There are intensely stunning films of most of Benitez's fights and most of the recent weeks, of course. And likewise, Benitez has been stunning Leonard.*]

"No problem, Liebling." He immediately reached down and grabbed the metal bar that joined the front two legs of G-S-G's chair and wrenched it as hard as he could up in the air. The result was that G-S-G was lifted and flipped backwards. The crowd around them jumped to their feet, and there was yells and spilled drinks and a few people picking themselves up off the floor. People behind craned to see what happened, people in front tried to get away. Before G-S-G was even off the floor, Gina and Vig had bolted.

[*Benitez trying to land with his left, throwing it, but not landing with it. Not often anyway. We've had one knock down. The flash knock-down in the third round, that I think embarrassed Rafael more than anything. Benitez fighting better in this round.*]

Vig and Gina sprinted out the same door that they had entered the Circus Maximus and made their way quickly through the gardens flanking the pool towards the door of the main hotel. The place was emptier than usual due to the fight, but a few people were still milling around.

[End of the round at hand, a better round for Benitez.]

Grey-Suit-Glasses had begun to catch up with them as they arrived at the hotel door but had slowed to a walk and was holding a white handkerchief to the side of his head. There were two security guards flanking the main doors; and one was speaking into his radio, seemingly struggling to be heard over the lobby hubbub.

[Sixth round action beginning! Rafael Benitez, now with an almost constant snare or leer on his face but giving the impression of coming on in the fourth round. His own left beginning to work. Looks longer in its action than Leonard's.]

Gina was beside Vig and didn't miss a step while gently tugging on his sleeve. "Follow me."

[He lost none of his confidence when he suffered that flash knockdown in the third round from a Leonard left. A very cautious Leonard as you can see. He is having trouble getting past Benitez's left, that's his problem right now.]

She guided them towards the right, passing across the main lobby, and after a quick glance to see if G-S-G had seen them, pushed open and slipped through one of the side 'staff-only' doors. Vig slipped through right behind her. It opened into a small concrete stairwell, with stairs going up to the hotel rooms and down to what Vig guessed was the parking garage. The air was cold and damp, not like the crisp dry air of the casino.

[Leonard is not able to mount an offense against the left of Benitez. A minute left to go. That was a good left by Leonard! Benitez attempted a counterpunch. Leonard has never gone past ten Rounds, keep that in mind.]

Vig peeked back through the door to the casino lobby. G-S-G was standing there, looking around, still dabbing the side of his head with his handkerchief. There was a small red mark on it, presumably blood.

[*Benitez has a cut! He has a severe cut! Look at this!*]

He didn't even look towards the door they had gone through. Vig gently closed the door and turned back towards Gina. To his surprise, she had headed up rather than down.

She called down to him as she disappeared up the stairwell. "He will think we are going to get a car, because that's what he would do."

[*Two minutes to go in this round. Now, Benitez must be cautious about a Leonard flurry from nowhere, when those dazzling quick hands suddenly deliver seven, eight, maybe ten blows.*]

Vig followed her up four flights to another set of double doors. She had taken two steps at a time, and never once broke her stride. When she got to the top floor, she pushed the two maintenance doors open to the warm evening sky. By the time he had made it out to the rooftop behind her, she was at the edge and was looking down at the street below. The sun was long gone, so the only lights were those from the hotels along the strip.

[*Seventh round action underway! Blood flowing again from Benitez's forehead. Terribly dangerous when that happens because it can endanger the vision. The blood is pouring down into his eyes. Blood in the mouth is a problem because it endangers breathing. The blood is coming right down the bridge of the nose and into the mouth. It would be a shame if the fight ended based on a headbutt.*]

Back before the helicopter tours, a rooftop view of the strip was something to behold. Straight in front of them across Las Vegas Boulevard was the bright pink sign for the Flamingo, next to a shorter squat sign for the Sands. Next door the brightly lit frontage for the Imperial Palace, with the distinctive blue roof with its oriental-style sign advertising Lovelace and the Mickey Finn Show... and the ubiquitous ninety-nine-cent steak.

[Two heads meeting, as you saw. And Benitez senses that he must strike and strike quickly! In trying to do so, he could leave himself open.]

Vig walked over beside her and looked down. Ceasers was set back from the main road, with gardens and arched patios set our front. The street was busy; it was still the place to be tonight even for those not attending the fight. He looked across at Gina. She was silhouetted against the light with her smiling face turned north towards Circus-Circus. You could still hear the crowd in the pavilion. It reminded him of the night they had seen Sinatra. She turned back toward him.

[Now of course, you know the rule. If this fight were to be stopped because of that butt, the fighter ahead of the scoring at the time of stoppage wins the fight.]

"What now Vig?"

"Whatever you want, Gina."

She laughed. "A drink. And I want to hear more about that German guy who saved our butts."

[The term is 'winner by technical decision...']

19 JEORG

Las Vegas, Nevada

Joerg was originally from Germany but had spent most of his twenties and thirties travelling around Europe. He was a nice, quiet, crazy bastard. The first time he travelled to Vegas he planned on doing only two things; "playing poker and banging hookers" (his words).

Vig had met him during a sojourn related to the former. He was a great poker player - not just by European standards - but by anyone's standards. Put him into a thousand-dollar game and he'd be the guy likely to double his stack in a few hours against most fields. When he announced to his buddies back home in Germany that he was planning his first trip to Vegas for a few weeks on his own, they gave him just one tip; if you see a good-looking girl in a casino bar, alone, dressed to kill and drinking; she is a working girl. Not 'probably', not 'almost certainly', but a complete lock to be looking for tricks.

Jeorg's travel plan was to stay in the nicest hotels he could find with a poker room, play enough ten-dollar-ante stud poker to get comped the room, and get laid at least once a day. The first few days went off without a hitch, making money on the felt, getting felt for his money.

He visited the Sands casino one night as the word was out

that some MLB guys had been spotted in the poker room and he wanted to go whale-hunting. He stopped for a drink at the bar beforehand and spotted this 'straight up nine' standing at the bar. The way he tells it, the barman brought Joerg his drink, slipping a white napkin neatly underneath it. The napkin had that pseudo-Arabic Sands logo imprinted upon it, matching the gigantic sign above the hotel, but more interestingly had what appeared to be a hand-written note on it that simply said "WHITE RUSSIAN" in black ink. Joerg called the barman over and asked him to make two White Russians, and to arrange a room in the hotel and bring him – discreetly – the key.

Not long after, two of the aforementioned drinks were ready and sitting on top of the bar right where the nine was standing. Joerg casually walked over to the end of the bar, sat down, and picked up one of the glasses, taking a small sip, waiting for her to make the first move.

"That's a shame."

Pause.

"What's a shame?"

"I thought both were for me."

Nice, thought Jeorg.

"You can have them both. I'm more of a Red Stripe drinker."

She took the drink out of his hand and spoke to the barman "A Red Stripe for my new friend here."

Joerg and the Nine hit it off like a house on fire. The way he tells it they were simpatico on every topic they discussed: life, gambling, poker, love, the best way to make a White Russian. Of course, in the back of his mind the whole time he was thinking that all this conversation was going to be added onto the meter. Out of the blue she asks the magic question. "Do you have a room here, or are you staying someplace else?"

He didn't need asking twice. After a short walk through the lobby and ride in the elevator, he opened the door to his brand-new untouched room and led her in. She didn't seem in the slightest bit perturbed by the fact that there was no sign at all of anyone staying in the room, he figured if she asked, he'd make something up in the moment. After turning on the light, he turned around to find her slipping off her dress. Christ. He smiled to himself, she was definitely a nine-and-a-half in this light.

He realized he still had no idea what this was going to cost him. He'd already spent an hour with her. It was the eighties, the beginning of the decade of decadence. There were certainly girls who cost under a c-note, but also girls who cost well over a grand. It was time to talk turkey, but how to open the topic while maintaining the illusion?

"Shouldn't we discuss money first?"

The look on her face made his stomach drop. She began hurriedly dressing, not embarrassed, just angry. Oh, shit.

"You're a fucking asshole."

"I'm sorry. I don't know what I was thinking."

"You thought I was a fucking prostitute. Jesus, we talked for an hour. You're an asshole."

She was already out the door and heading down the corridor before Jeorg could even move. Of course he ran after her, but she wouldn't even turn around. He had blown it.

When Joerg told Vig this story a few years later, his reply – when he stopped laughing - was just one question "How long before you hired a real call girl?"

"It was about two hours. I told them to send me a ten."

20 TONY

4041 Audrie Street
December 1st, 1979
(early morning)

[Benitez trying to come on now. Benitez sparring with a good left earlier. Connected with a right and Leonard felt it! We're down to twenty minutes remaining in the fight. Two great young professional fighters. Masters of their craft. Look at them going at it standing toe to toe! Leonard trying to chop Benitez down. Benitez is frowning in pain.]

Even though they both knew there was a chance that they wouldn't get paid, the imminent winning of their bet was still a cause for celebration. "And here's to your hundred and twenty thousand dollars, wherever it is!" Gina raised her glass again and drained it.

"There'll be a cut for you too – you put up collateral."

"Yep, that's why I left out the five." She glanced at the television in the corner of the bar that was showing the end of the fight, then looked at Vig seriously for a moment. "What are you going to do now? Who was that guy Sacco?"

Sacco was a character, and Vig knew him mainly by reputation for several years. He made it his business to avoid spending time with bookies and gamblers outside of those he met through boxing, but everyone in Vegas knew who Sacco was.

The 'Organized Crime Control Act' of October 1970 was enacted after the Valachi hearings blew the lid off organized gambling and racketeering in the United States. While the wise guys worried about RICO, the gamblers worried about OCCA. Sacco had been arrested with his partner just one year later after they had been double-crossed by one of their own, and because of that - and Nixon's hard-on for jailing gamblers - he went inside for a short stretch. Vig heard he had done three years.

[Leonard going after him. He can go fifteen rounds... he sure has proved it today! Unless by a miracle he gets knocked out... and yes Benitez can go fifteen rounds.]

Vig decided to spare Gina the details, but he knew better than to outright lie. "I know him from my days working at fights in L.A. and San Diego."

"Was he the guy you owed money to?"

Vig shook his head. "Never."

"So... why was he trying to run us down... is he trying to rob you or something? C'mon Vig..."

[And there's going to be a winner and there's going to be a loser. These young men are fighters. There... he got him down again. It seemed almost inevitable! Look at him; rubber-legged, wobbly, looking at the crowd!]

Vig tried to explain to Gina that the most valuable thing he handled was information. The truth was that Sacco probably didn't care who won the lousy fight – he was probably as clued into the fix as Vig was – all he wanted to know was who had leaked the information. It had certainly affected the price, and if Sacco was in on it and trying to make money out of it, whoever had leaked it had cost him money, potentially a lot of money.

It was possible that he was not in on it directly, but had lost money himself (one way or another) and was seeking to get himself even (one way or another). This was ironically reassuring, as Vig had a reputation as a tombstone; he never talked about his bets or the fights that he got involved in. At least he hadn't up to today.

[Alright, let him do it… it doesn't dilute the courage he showed or the skills he showed! Maybe now they won't call Sugar Ray Leonard a hype.]

Tony interrupted them. "Call for you Vig."

Vig looked around. He was placing a telephone on the bar. This wasn't good. "Who is it?"

"He said you'll know. Sorry Vig." He looked genuinely upset that he had to break his own reputation for discretion. Vig reached over and picked up the receiver while trying to avoid eye contact with Gina.

"Who is this?"

The line was not very clear.

"I'm sorry about this Vig."

"I hear that a lot. Sorry about what?"

For a minute, he didn't recognize the voice. Then his stomach sank. It was Chuck the bookie. He didn't bother introducing himself. "It was just business, I owed Sacco money, or at least he thought I did, and the only way to get off the hook was to tell him where I got my information."

Vig's eyes flicked to Gina. He had to ask, but he wasn't sure he wanted the answer. "Did she know?"

She seemed to understand. Her eyes widened. The voice at the other end of the line seemed hesitant. "She's a mutual friend, Victor. I bring business her way, she brings business mine. She didn't know that I'd… what would happen. Neither did I at the time."

"So, your plan was to tip him off that I had inside info on the fight… in return for what, exactly? Any why did he give a shit who fixed the fight?"

"Because he thought that it was fixed the other way."

This was a new one on him. Who had managed to persuade Sacco that Sugar Ray was going to take a fall? The price on Benitez was long at plus three hundred so Sacco must have been thinking that it was going to be fucking triple Christmas. Vig wondered how much he had lost, and whom he had lost it to.

Then it hit him. Chuck the bookie.

He spoke slowly and softly. "So how much did you take off Sacco?"

He laughed, he laughed right down the phone at him. "Not as much as you think. I took that bet fair and square Vig. I gave him two-sixty when the strip was paying two-ninety, but he still took everything I would give him. I guess I should have figured something was up."

"When did you decide to throw me under the bus?"

"Vig, come on. That's not how it was."

"OK, let's have it your way. Here's another question; where's my one hundred and twenty-five thousand dollars?"

He must have known the question was coming, but he still pretended to be surprised by it.

"I have to leave town for a while. Sacco is mad about the loss and seems to think he can take a mulligan on this bet."

"I'm starting to agree with him."

"Don't be like that Vig. I have your money, and you have my word that you'll get it someday. I was planning on semi-retiring anyway. Ever been to Oregon, Vig?"

"Let me make this very clear. Don't leave town with one red cent of my fucking money."

"I'm afraid it's a little late for that. I'm already out of Clark County, calling from a place you might know in Pahrump. Please don't have hard feelings. You have my word you will get your one-twenty-five, but I have some family business to attend to first."

Vig knew it was fruitless, but he gave it one last shot anyway. "If Sacco thinks you've set him up, there won't be too many places he cannot reach."

Vig needn't have bothered. "Mr. Sacco and I have an understanding. He seems to think that someone set him up on this bet, and that you know who that person is. He may be right." A noise in the background interrupted him. Vig couldn't make it out. "I have to go, Vig. Remember, you have my word about the money. I pay my bettors, but it might be a while. Give my best to Miss Gina." He hung up the phone.

There was a pause. Vig waited for Gina to speak. She didn't wait too long. "Whatever he told you Vig, you know I wouldn't help anyone rip you off. I just referred wealthy johns to him when they were trying to get a little off-strip action, and he did the same."

Vig didn't know what to believe, but he couldn't really conceive that she was in on it. Maybe he was being naïve, but it just wasn't her style. She was an adventurer, not a fool. He decided to trust her.

"I know, Gina."

They both stared into their drinks for a moment. It wasn't the money. It was never really about the money (even though this hit stung more than a little) it was the fact that he'd gotten mixed up in some sort of hazing for two rich dickheads, traded info with an off-strip bookie against his own better judgment, and placed a bet in cash and credit with a bookie he didn't know. Gina made him do strange things. Or maybe Vig made himself do strange things when she was around.

"If he found us, how do we know Sacco's guys won't?"

Vig ignored her and turned to Tony. "Two more beers."

"Vig, come on… are we safe here?"

"Is there anyone else coming for us, Tony?"

Tony began fixing the drinks. "I think you're alright here Vig. No locals cut up in this gaff, especially when I'm working. I guess that's why you were here in the first place."

There are many ways to rekindle a relationship. Losing his entire net worth on a winning bet is one way of doing it. While Tony had been speaking, an idea had been forming. However, two more people had questions to answer. He smiled.

"And two daiquiris." Tony nodded. "One more thing Tony… ever hear of a local degenerate called Murray?"

21 COFFEE

Av. 12 (Calle 54), San Jose, Costa Rica
August 1985
(six years later)

The taxi ride from Alajuela to San Jose should have taken forty minutes, but regularly took seventy. This was partly due to the shitty traffic, partly due to the shitty roads, but also because Vig preferred to go via Heredia, north of the city. The roads were smoother, and it was easier to sleep until they got to the heavier traffic. By the time they crossed over the Ria Torres and approached the Parque La Sabana, he was almost awake.

Vig leaned forward and spoke to the driver "Parar aquí, por un momento".

The driver knew the drill and pulled over beside a small kiosk tucked in at the corner of the park. A few coins later and Vig held two small steaming paper cups, ducked back into the car and handed one of the cups to the driver. He figured that if you were forced to live in Costa Rica, you might as well get to enjoy the coffee.

"Pura vida."

"Pura vida."

Vig sat into the front passenger seat, while the driver – still holding the cup in one hand - swung the car back on to the road and drove the last three hundred yards to the office. Another few Colones and Vig was out on the path and in the door. Turning right to the stairwell, he climbed the four flights of steps and came to a very nondescript reception area. Beyond reception was a bank of small desks, all empty but one, and on the right-hand wall several small glass offices. Vig waved to Carole; he was the second one in to work as usual, after the ever-diligent office manager. He made his way around to one of the glass offices – his own office – and took his seat behind the desk. Above him, a fan rotated slowly. Vig was grateful for even the smallest movement of air, silently thanking her for switching it on when she had come in.

He was halfway through his coffee when the first call came, He banged the bottom of the receiver in a well-practiced move and the phone jumped up into his hand.

"Hello."

It was Carole on the other end of the line. "I have a new account request, looking for credit."

The early bird. "Why is this being put through to me?"

"She asked for you by name. Victor Green."

That was strange for two reasons. First; nobody outside San Jose knew that he was here. They were still a pretty new outfit. Second; the handful of prospects he had reached out to before starting work here had been given a pseudonym. Third; it was a girl. That was typically a sign of a player whose account has been closed for bad credit or insider betting using his wife or girlfriend to circumvent the ban.

"Put her through."

"Sure thing Vig."

There was a short pause, and a click. The line wasn't great, which was unusual as they had good international PBX lines, so anything that came from the US was clear unless it was from a payphone or a carphone. They had plenty of customers who regularly used both.

"Hello." (they didn't identify the company over the phone, even to repeat customers).

"Hello, is that Vig?"

Jesus Christ. Some voices you never forget. His throat went dry.

After a pause. "Are you there, Vig?"

He swallowed and managed to get out two words. "Hi Gina."

A sigh – perhaps of relief – came from the other end of the phone. "Good to hear your voice. How long is it since you've seen me?"

"That's an unusual way to ask that question, even for you. Where are you? Doesn't sound like you are in the US." His heart was beating.

"I'm right across the road from where you picked up those two coffees. Are you free for lunch?"

22 PHONE CALL

25th December 1979

Vig looked at Gina one more time to check if she was ready. She nodded.

"Hillcrest Country Club please."

"Whom shall I say is calling?"

"Victor Green. I'm looking for Mister Carmine Yanuck."

"I'm not sure if he's in the club today. I'll page him."

"I'll wait."

A few more minutes went by, then the phone was picked up.

"I hear you had some problems in Las Vegas, Mister Green."

Vig didn't recognize the voice, but he figured if this guy knew who he was, he may as well press on. "How is the movie business going?"

"My father decided not to proceed with the venture. Too many complications."

"Life is full of complications. Who am I speaking to?"

"This is Mr. Yanuck's son, Richard. I can speak for him."

"I have a loose end to tie up. Two of your boys ran a small tab in a local Nevada establishment. I have a minor cashflow issue at the moment, so would appreciate if you could give the manager some assurances that you will take care of the tab."

Richard was – as could be expected – really fucking confused. "What are you talking about?"

Vig handed the phone to Gina. "Hello again. This is the proprietress of the restaurant at the Salt Wells Villas. There's a seventy-dollar tab that your two associates left. Can I add this tab to your fathers?"

There was a low mumble on the phone. Gina handed the receiver back to Vig. The voice on the other end remained calm. "It seems the trusted bookie and the trusted madam are not so trustworthy anymore."

"Trust is earned. Your father used to respect that. I am going to assume that you know who Ronald Sacco is, and what he is capable of. I am also going to assume your father knows the risks in getting his name associated with fight fixing and off-track bookmaking. I am guessing that whatever money Chuck stole from him is a drop in the ocean. I am not asking you to compensate me, nor am I going to threaten you or Carmine. I am especially not going to beg. My friend here has a bill of account for her licensed Nevada business, and now that I have furnished her with your father's real name, home, office, and club address... she has the legally protected right to pursue payment. Publicly."

"You think a bill from a whorehouse is going to damage my father's reputation?"

"We all need to move on from this. We both have no interest in loose ends."

Richard laughed. "You obviously haven't heard the news. My father passed away three days ago... from throat cancer. I think you can be pretty sure that there will be no further business and tell your cathouse friend that this bill... along with the many, many others... will remain unpaid."

23 MURRAY

3801 Las Vegas Boulevard South
14th December 1979

Three card monte has never gone away. It used to be a staple around army bases, factories, train stations and tourist traps all around the United States. It attracted all kinds of degenerates and conmen, and Murray proved to be no different. It had taken Vig three days to eventually find him, working as a shill and spotter for a three-card-monte game near one of the off-strip construction sites. Vig simply walked up and collared him. Murray didn't even see Vig until he was practically on top of him. He let him finish his day's work and agreed to meet him later at the Trop.

Vig had already resigned himself to the fact that he was never going to see much of his money again, so figured that the best thing for him to do was put Murray to work as a runner. Vig had a roll to build, and that meant bookmaking, and the best runners were the ones who did the least thinking.

Of course Murray had other ideas. When Vig arrived in the Trop that evening, Murray was standing at a craps table in the pit. He claimed to be broke, but he still managed to insist on making him watch him bet on the field beside every come-out roll like an asshole.

"I got a line on something big, Vig."

"I don't need anything other than to get some bets down, and you're going to be my runner."

"Nah I'm serious. I got something big right here." - he gestured to the dealer – "the Kansas City mob are selling this place."

"Yep, I read the papers."

"What you didn't read in the papers is that the boss who is taking the skim isn't happy and wants to get paid off before the deal goes through."

Well, of course he did. Nobody liked a free income stream being cut off. Vig waited for Murray to get to the point but it didn't seem like it was happening any time soon. Murray shot craps like a real degenerate. He insisted on covering all the numbers and wouldn't leave a table until he had them all working at once. With a sawbuck on the pass line he'd take the full odds, so one bad streak could easily burn through a grand in a few minutes. A fun time, but a bad habit.

Between rolling dice and yelling for more drinks, Vig eventually managed to get the bones of Murray's idea. The KC mob boss who oversaw taking and distributing the skim was apparently wetting his beak a little too much. This was one of the reasons that they were selling the property; their income had dropped. This mob boss had hatched a plan to take a little out of the kitty before the sale; he probably felt entitled after all the hard work he hadn't done over the years.

According to Murray, the plan was simple; the boss was going to push a load of markers through the books with fake names, that would never be collected, and pocket the cash. To get the markers approved he had a deal with one of the Irish pit-bosses who was planning on leaving Vegas to return home once the place closed. The pit boss would be blacklisted, and possibly under police investigation, but he would have a generous 'severance' in his pocket paid for by the Ramada buyers (assuming his split with the boss was favorable and would be honored).

"What's the angle for us?"

"The pit boss has no idea who will be writing the markers. His instructions are simply to approve every marker made out for exactly two-and-a-half thousand dollars during his Monday shift. Monday night is the only night of the week that the head cashier is off work, so he doesn't need to get them countersigned. They'll sit there all night in a locked box, and nobody will know there are dozens of them until the following night, by which time Irish will be half-way to Tipperary or wherever the fuck. All we do is pull up a seat when we know this guy is on shift and ask for a marker for exactly two thousand five hundred dollars. We can do it four times, get them all paid, and pull out ten thousand each."

Vig was doubtful. Firstly, casinos were not stupid. They knew they were a target for marker fraud right before they shut or before staff quit. Secondly, the dealers in his pit will know something is up after seeing a bunch of identical markers come across the felt at that frequency and could easily report it. Too many people.

"I know what you're thinking Vig. It's all figured out. He's got a coachload of Jap tourists lined up to write the markers. They'll have a host come in and order drinks, make a big noise, and the dealers and other bosses will think they have a big line of credit for the whole group. They'll take those big quarters and burn off about five hundred to a grand each. Some will win of course, the idea is to try and get two grand out for each marker, maybe four markers per jap. Twenty japs, that's one hundred and fifty grand for the mob boss plus ten for the Irish pit-boss to send him on his way the following morning."

It was a smart plan. It would feel like any other day-tripping junket of businessmen taking a break from the conference or the pool. The host would have to be fake, as a host would be chased for a bunch of bad markers as much as the players. But they'd only have to fool the dealers, and only for a short time, and a dealer would only make a stink if they thought they could be under suspicion themselves. Dealers never want cheaters to tip too big.

"How do you get to hear about this? If you've heard, others

have heard. Especially with that many involved."

"That's the best part, Vig. The fake junket is a bunch of circus guys visiting San Diego on their day off. They don't speak English, but they know how to gamble and they're getting fifty bucks each on the bus back that night. They won't even shut off the engine, it will sit in the parking lot and they'll all file back onto the bus and turn the chips over to the driver, getting paid fifty dollars in cash."

"They'll never get that volume of chips turned into cash without raising eyebrows."

"They will. They'll be sold to the I.P. at ninety cents on the dollar and they'll just move them through their normal nightly chip exchange."

"Why would the I.P. do something like this?"

"Because the owner - Ralph Engelstad - hates the fucking Ramada for some reason."

And how do you know all this?

"Me and Ralph go way back."

"Bullshit Murray. Why would a multi-millionaire get involved with a degenerate like you?"

"We share a hobby."

24 IRISH

3801 Las Vegas Boulevard South
18th December 1979

The marker system in Las Vegas is simple. If you have cash in the bank, you can get credit at a casino. In fact, if you have cash in the bank you can usually get credit at every casino. Nowadays there are a handful of rewards programs linking casinos together, and you cannot double-dip. But back in the seventies you could have credit at multiple casinos at the same time based on the same roll. While they would claim to share this information, if they suspected you were a whale, they would keep it to themselves.

Irish's shift was due to start at ten and run straight through till one the next day, then he was due on a flight from L.A. to London. Their plan was to go to the pit, sit down, play a little blackjack, and see what transpired. Murray wanted to wear disguises, but Vig refused to call attention to himself.

They arrived at 4am when things were quiet. As they walked through the ranks of slot machines to the table games Vig surveyed the place. There was still a little action in the pit, the Christmas revelers had started to arrive in town and were whooping it up at a couple of tables. There were a few seats occupied at each of the low stakes blackjack tables, and further

119

along there were six empty medium and high-stakes tables arranged in a rectangle facing outward, and a large middle-aged pit boss in a tuxedo stood in the middle of the rectangle, looking out over the tables. If this was their guy, and this was the night, then there was no sign of nervousness or anything untoward about him. Attentive, but not paying attention to anything in particular. Murray dropped back until he was beside Vig and whispered 'That's him. That's Irish."

Vig was still dubious. "Let's shoot a little craps first."

Murray didn't need asking twice. They took a spot at the rail either side of one of the five-dollar tables. Vig let Murray chase his boxes with the couple of hundred dollars walking around money he had. They needn't have been so cautious. Nothing happened apart from one of the players at the lower-stakes blackjack table standing up and leaving, with a nice stack of green twenty-five-dollar chips. Most importantly from Vig's perspective, nobody seemed to recognize either of them.

After a couple of dozen rolls which were heavy on the nines putting both of them a couple of hundred each up, it was time to move to Irish's pit. They sat down at a fifty-dollar blackjack table where the dealer was shuffling the single deck. The pit boss didn't appear to notice them, but Vig was sure he did. Vig brought out three hundred in green chips and put them in front of him. "Let's see how this goes for starters."

Murray wasn't so patient. He seemed to forget he had four hundred or so on him in cash and chips, and immediately told the dealer he wanted a marker. Irish was instantly beside the table. "Name?"

Murray didn't hesitate to use a fake name. "Marcus Wells."

"How much are you looking for Mr. Wells?"

To Murray's credit, he didn't hesitate this time either. "Two thousand five hundred dollars. Two yellows, ten blacks and twenty greens. The greens are lucky for me so far tonight."

The pit boss had a marker slip in his hand, and carefully wrote out the name and amount. He asked the dealer and Murray to countersign, and said "One moment, sir." He stepped back to his desk and appeared to check a list, then lifted a phone.

The worst that could happen at this point was that he would check the name, see it was not cleared for credit, and then ask Murray i.e. 'Mr. Wells' to explain himself in the office. Murray would bluster something about his host not calling ahead, apologize, and they'd both leave.

Vig needn't have worried. Irish stepped back to the table after about twenty seconds and it was done; he signed the slip himself, handed the counterfoil to Murray, and put five yellow chips in front of Murray on the felt, ignoring Murray's request. "Good luck sir." It was as simple as that.

Irish was expecting them to play a little then head for the cashier, and Vig and Murray had agreed to stick to that plan. Of course, Murray had other ideas.

"All yellows? Fine." He pushed the entire stack into the box in front of him. "Let's play."

The dealer looked up "Yellows in play." The pit boss didn't even turn around.

This was how it was going to be. Of course, Murray won. He parlayed that twenty-five hundred into ten grand in two hands. Then split the stack in two and played two boxes with five grand on each. One lost, the other won. He did the same again and both hands lost. Three minutes in and he was felted.

Vig hadn't even played a hand yet. He looked over at the pit boss, who was standing back at his post. Without a word he began to walk back over with a marker in his hand. He didn't go through the theatre of calling it in this time, just laid it on the felt and got Murray and the dealer to sign it, pulling another five yellows out and putting them in front of Murray.

This was going to end badly for someone. Vig had taken steps the previous evening to ensure it ended badly for nobody but Murray.

25 RALPH

Thunderbird Airstrip
Sometime in 1964

The problem with guys like Murray, is that they talk a lot, and they leave a trail wherever they go. To stay in business the trick is to spend more time listening then talking, and spend more time earning favors than owing them. Murray thought that he knew everyone as well as anyone. What Murray didn't know was that Victor Green and Ralph Engelstad had become acquainted several years beforehand, and Vig could count him among those who owed him a favor.

In the mid-sixties Ralph had put together a beautiful land deal. He had bought the Thunderbird Field airstrip and began acquiring plots around it a few miles northwest of the Las Vegas strip. After only two years holding the empty lot he had sold the airstrip and about one hundred and fifty acres around it to Howard Hughes and parlayed that cash into the Kona Kai.

While Vig had never visited the strip before 1969, he had been briefly within sight of it five years before. He had been sent down to hand over cash to a gambler previously unknown to him who was owed money by a boxing promoter in San Diego. A gambler and businessman by the name of Ralph Engelstad.

Vig didn't know any details, just that the promoter owed Mr. Engelstad money, and for some reason this payment needed to get into his hands quickly. Vig didn't care, he was getting paid five hundred to accompany a bag on a light aircraft on the short trip from Burbank to Thunderbird Field. Vig was due to meet Engelstad at the airstrip, hand him the bag, climb back on the plane and fly back to Burbank. The pilot was supposed to stop, shut the passenger side engine off so Vig could hop out and make the handover, then wait for him to hop back in and off they'd go. The trip down in the plane was uneventful, the pilot was a charter, and apparently not talkative or interested in the reason for the unusual trip.

When they landed, there were two men standing beside each other at the airstrip. One of them was Engelstad (Vig had been given a photograph to ensure he could identify him) and the other was someone else he recognized; a well-known gambler by the name of Barnett Magids.

Of course, it did not go down as planned. The minute the plane stopped on the tarmac the pilot cut both engines, turned to Vig and said, "You know who that is?"

"Yep." Vig hoped a simple answer would suffice.

"Is that who we are here to meet?"

"It's who I'm here to meet. Can you open the door?"

The pilot leaned across the passenger seat and popped the door handle. Vig climbed out and made the small jump to the tarmac, but to his surprise the pilot quickly followed him out the small squat hatch and jumped down on the tarmac, jogging over to the taller of the two men before Vig got a chance to speak. "It's a pleasure to meet you Mr. Magids."

Magids seemed to look right through him, paused for a second, turned to face Vig and asked, with a polite tone "You have something for us?"

Vig suppressed any reaction and focused on the job. This Magids guy was not part of the plan.

"I have a delivery for this gentleman here." Vig gestured to Engelstad, who remained silent.

Magids seemed annoyed by the comment. "I am his business partner. We are here to collect."

The plane engine had fallen quiet, and the three other men were now standing in a row, facing Vig. Engelstad stood with his shoulders slumped, not looking down but not making eye contact. The pilot and Magids were focused on Vig. It didn't take a genius to figure out that something was off here. During a cash handover like this, Vig typically had a backup plan, but this time with the touch-and-go airport drop he didn't have anything solid.

He raised his voice. "You here to collect, Mr. Engelstad?"

Silence.

Magids spoke "He sure is here to collect. Go get the bag." He gestured to the pilot.

Vig raised his voice. "Don't fucking touch the bag. I want to hear him say it."

The pilot and Magids looked at each other, and the pilot began to walk towards the cockpit. The trouble with heists that are witnessed, is that the victim starts to catch some of the blame, or at least some of the suspicion. Most heists of money-in-transit were inside jobs, and this looked like it was going to be something similar. These guys' plan was clearly to get Vig to handover the cash to them and leave. Something was up, and Vig had to try and rescue the situation one way or the other.

The pilot was climbing back out of the cockpit with the small sports holdall in his hand. Engelstad didn't react. He didn't seem to be looking at anything in particular. Vig guessed that he had been drugged by these pieces of shit, and now they were going to boost his money.

Sometimes you need complexity and sophistication to get out of these types of situations. But this time the trick was a simple one. Generally, when you deliver cash for someone, they don't count it when they give it to you... they know how much is in there because they put it there. The guy who collects it doesn't count it either. If it's short then the sender gets a call, and if the runner has been light-fingered then they get dealt with accordingly. It was unlikely the pilot or this shithead Magids would open the duffel bag and look at the money. Why bother? If it wasn't there, they weren't going to send Vig back to San Diego to get it.

Even if they did, there was twenty grand in wrapped tens sitting right there to pass a cursory inspection. The rest was in the lining of Vig's coat... twenty-three slabs of hundreds just sitting in the poacher's pockets.

Standing there facing them on the tarmac, he wondered why they had gone to the trouble of bringing Engelstad to the drop off at all. They probably hoped that Vig would toss them the bag no questions asked and fly right back, not wishing to get himself mixed up in any trouble. Vig was wondering whether this actually might have worked, when he saw a pair of headlights flash in the distance.

The pilot must have seen Vig's gaze shift, as he turned around and spotted them too, gesturing to Magids. They didn't seem surprised, they just stepped back quickly towards the plane, leaving Engelstad behind standing on the tarmac.

Magids was almost laughing as the pilot fired up the engines. "When Ralph's friends show up, please explain to them what happened to the money."

Vig watched the headlights get closer. "I'll be sure and do that."

The twin propeller engines roared, and the plane began to pivot back towards the runway. For the first time, Ralph Engelstad moved. He turned his head toward the noise but seemed unsteady on his feet, and just sat down cross-legged on the ground right where he had been standing. By the time the headlights had arrived the plane was leaving the runway in the distance.

The car was a black dodge, with slightly tinted windows, and came to a halt right beside the slumped figure. Vig expected several figures to jump out, but just the driver's door opened, and a tall man in a black and white slim-fitting suit stepped out. He took a look at the slumped figure on the ground before turning to look at the now distant plane, his hand over his eyes.

He didn't bother turning to face Vig. "Could you give me a hand here?"

Vig didn't hesitate. The two of them lifted the semi-prone Ralph by his shoulders and placed him in the back of the car. The driver didn't say a word while this was happening, but when Ralph was belted into his seat, he stood up and appeared to notice Vig properly for the first time. "Thanks for that. Now, I need to know what the hell happened here."

"He's been doped, 'ludes probably. He was brought out here to be robbed."

He seemed like he wasn't surprised. "The Magids guy?"

"Yep."

"Where did you come from? You come in on the bird?"

"San Diego. Yep."

"Perfect. He needs to sober up, and that's where we are going. Want a ride back?"

They drove all the way back to San Diego. It took a little over six hours. Ralph in the back, asleep behind a screen, with Vig sitting beside the driver up front, over two hundred thousand dollars stuffed into his coat. Vig had decided that he wouldn't say anything about the money until he could talk to Ralph directly. The driver didn't talk much, so Vig had time to figure out exactly what he was going to say. He wasn't particularly concerned about his safety - despite what had gone on earlier - he just wanted to get the money handed over, explain the shortfall, and get the hell home.

By the time they got to the outskirts of the city, Ralph had begun to wake up. Vig could just about see him in the mirror, he was still slumped against the window, but his eyes had begun to slowly open.

Vig was wondering if he was just going to lie there awake for the rest of the ride, but he suddenly sat up straight quickly, straightened his tie, and looked around him.

"Where am I Tommy?"

"On your way back to the apartment, boss."

"Who is that with you in the front seat?"

"This is the guy who was sent to deliver your money in Vegas."

"What happened?"

"What do you remember?"

"I went back to the suite at the Riviera with that bookie and a few girls, and we drank some champagne… or something."

"You got spiked, sir." He side-eyed Vig. "With some sort of Quaaludes most likely."

"That's sure as hell what it feels like, Tommy." He was straightening his tie and slicking back his hair. He didn't seem too surprised at the situation he found himself in.

He looked pointedly at Vig. "What's your story?"

"They took you along to pick up the money. The pilot who flew me was in on it and he knew the bookie. The bookie's name was Magids by the way. He's not really a bookie, more of a sharp."

He looked dejected. "I guess that's two hundred and fifty grand I'm light with no way of getting it back. I hope I don't have to sell the airstrip or one of the houses to keep the lights on at home."

Vig allowed himself a smile as he reached into the inside of his coat.

26 MARKER

3801 Las Vegas Boulevard South
18th December 1979

Vig had to get Murray out of the way for a few minutes to make this work. He never left the tables and was always quick taking a leak. Probably didn't wash his hands. But Vig had come prepared. As Murray stood up, Vig put his hand on his arm to stop him and stuck out his other hand for Murray to shake.

"Murray, it looks like you came through on this one after all. I should never have doubted you."

Murray looked surprised, but happy.

He put his hand in Vig's, and his expression changed as he realized that Vig had palmed him a little polythene bag with a gram-and-a-half or so of white powder in it. A smile crossed his lips. He turned on his heel and headed back to the bathroom, practically skipping.

When he came back, he had clearly done a heavy bump and was visibly wired, but he kept his shit together. Vig was counting on it. Murray promptly went on a heater and ran his next twenty-five hundred up to two big dimes and he couldn't have been happier. He started going south every now and then, pocketing a yellow or two, but was getting lucky enough to keep about twenty grand in front of him pretty consistently. No more markers needed, and that suited Vig just fine.

In the meantime, Vig had been keeping a low profile, but what Murray didn't know was that while he'd been in the can Vig had asked Irish to write him six markers for twenty-five hundred each. While he was asking for them, the dealer made a point of looking down and counting her stacks. Vig guessed it was better she looked anywhere rather than at the federal crime that Irish and Vig were committing right there on the felt beside her. Irish didn't even pause. He brought the book of markers and filled in and counter-signed all six before he even put them in front of Vig, then slid out a stack each of yellow and black. Fifteen thousand dollars exactly.

Irish spoke softly to Vig. "You want to try another table?"

"What?"

"If you move to another table to change your luck; you can come back to me for another fifteen g's later."

"I'll keep that in mind."

Vig looked down at the markers and began filling them in.

'Name: Murray Wilson'. A scrawl for a signature.

Irish looked at him for a second, then looked towards Murray who was walking back from the can, oblivious to their transaction.

"Is there a problem?"

"No problem Mr. Wilson" he practically winked. "I've got that next fifteen waiting if you don't get lucky."

Murray slid onto his chair. "Deal me in!"

That's how things proceeded for the next hour. Murray kept his heater of a lifetime going, going south with nickels every now and then while betting them in fistfuls. It was incredible. The dealer they had started with had been switched out, and the new dealer was happy to take the black and yellow tokes. He didn't even notice what Vig was betting.

Every time Murray went to the can, Vig wrote another six markers and pocketed another ten grand, keeping five on the table. Every marker had Murray's real name on it. He could do this a total of six times in two hours because Murray kept stepping out to take another bump.

By the end of the session Vig estimated that Murray had pocketed maybe thirty grand and had a little more than that in front of him. A heater, and free coke to boot. At the same time, Vig himself had pocketed sixty thousand in cash, and dusted off the other thirty.

The dealer was washing the decks between shoes when they heard the first of the tourists approaching the pit behind them. It was time to leave, but Vig knew it was not going to be easy to pry a wired Murray away from a hot table "Time to split, Mr. Wells."

Of course, Murray had forgotten his fake name. "What are you talking about Vig… who the fuck is Mister Wells?"

The dealer glanced up, but just for a second.

Vig grabbed Murray's lapel and drew him close. "You're a fucking idiot, Mr. Wells."

The seats beside them were beginning to fill up. Wherever they had found their Japanese fake-marker-writer-tourists, they seemed legit.

"Come on Vig, a few more hands."

"We've got to go. Now." The table was suddenly full. There was some cash being exchanged for chips, probably cover before they started cutting markers.

Vig turned to the dealer and gestured to his stacks, practically throwing the chips from his pocket onto the felt "Swap those for plaques."

Vig tossed her a yellow for herself. To her credit, she was already cutting stacks of twenty chips and preparing to change him up before it had even hit the toke box.

"Don't fucking cash me out." Murray yelled. The tourists at the table were beginning to look at us. "You go Vig. I'm staying right here."

Vig looked from Murray to the dealer. Irish had the marker book in his hand and hadn't noticed any commotion yet. Fuck it, Murray was on his own. Vig rolled off the stool and headed straight for the cashier with his pile of plaques. Thankfully there was no line.

"Good evening Sir. You want to box it or cash out?"

"Cash please." Any other day he would have had it put on deposit at the cage, but the doors were closing, and the chips would be worthless soon, certainly when attached to someone who wrote bad markers on camera.

"I don't know if we have that much cash on hand. I'll just be a moment."

Vig knew that was bullshit. The cashier was probably skimming the cage himself, knowing the place was closing. Sometimes this town really stank.

"I just want six slabs, buddy How about you just give me back six of the ten I bought in with?"

That speeded things up a little. Cashiers knew never to piss off a whale, or else the whale's host might ensure it was their last shift. "No problem, Sir."

Vig took his slabs – bundles of currency still wrapped in the little paper ribbon - and put one in each pocket. Trouser front, trouser back, left, right, both sides of jacket. This was more out of habit than anything else.

Rather than go by the main door, he left the Tropicana via the parking lot and made his way over to the Pacifica, then left by their lot and headed up north on Koval Lane towards the back of the MGM. It was a chilly night, so the streets were relatively empty, despite the holiday season. Vig could almost see his breath in front of him.

Vig felt a brief blush of guilt for leaving Murray behind. It was possible that Murray would be fine on his own. Or dead. Or something in between. Hopefully not something in between.

27 HERR GRÜN

3535 Las Vegas Boulevard South
April 20th 1980

"Name, please?"

Vig had offered to make his own way down to the hotel to attend the party, but Ralph had insisted on sending a car to collect him. The car had pulled into the underground parking lot, which was flanked by two security staff, one holding a clipboard and one speaking softly into a walkie-talkie. The car pulled up right at the door. Before he had even stepped out, he was asked for his name.

"Victor Green."

The guy with the clipboard studied his face and checked the list carefully, eventually ticking off what was presumably his name.

"Welcome Mr. Green. Please come this way."

Vig was led through the doorway to a small service elevator. The guy never left his side. As they rode the elevator Vig took the opportunity to size up his temporary companion. He had a blonde military haircut and was dressed in the standard black security suit and tie, with the walkie-talkie strapped to his belt. He didn't seem like the normal vegas security guard type, he was younger and – frankly – in better shape. Vig guessed that a guy like Ralph Engelstad would have his own private security detail not just the standard casino floor meatheads.

They ascended about ten floors, and stepped out into another short corridor, at the end of which was another door with another – female – security guard standing outside. Blondie stayed in the elevator and headed back down, and the girl opened the door behind her and gestured for Vig to step in in front of her. "Mr. Green. Right this way."

Vig had seen a lot of shit in his time, but nothing prepared him for what was waiting on the other side.

The thing about a hotel conference room full of Nazi memorabilia is, that you don't really register what it is at first. The room was big and was decked out like a movie set. Anschluss-style red white and black swastika flags hung on the walls. A half-dozen mannequins in German army gear dotted around the room. There were about thirty or forty other people in the room, mostly couples and small groups of men, each dressed sharply and each holding a drink. Some had cocktails, but many of the men and a few of the women were holding metal steins of foamy yellow beer.

There were small softly lit plinths dotted around the room that seemed to have books and other paperwork spread out under the glass. Vig stepped to the nearest unattended one and took a look at what was on display. It seemed to be two separate sets of identification papers for one person, placed alongside each other. The face in the pictures did not look like the model of typical Aryan perfection, it was a sallow-faced dark haired man.

When he looked closer, Vig realized it was two different men, twin brothers, named Maksim and Vassilis Hatzipanigis. He couldn't understand any of the text on the papers apart from two dates inscribed on each set – March 11th, 1919 and February 4th, 1938. Whoever these two were, they seem to have been born on the same day and also appeared to have signed up for the German army on the same day, aged eighteen.

Vig was wondering the significance of this when he felt a presence at his shoulder. He turned to see Ralph Engelstad himself standing there in a black uniform, with narrow silver-braided shoulder boards on the jacket.

"Good evening, Mister Green, or should I say, Herr Grün?" he chuckled.

"Mr. Engelstad, good evening. And thank you for sending the car. Unnecessary but appreciated."

"Not trying to be showy, Herr Grün. It is a matter of the utmost discretion. This particular gathering is not for everyone."

"Well, I guess it is nice to be part of your circle, Mr. Engelstad."

"You were looking at the papers of my two uncles?"

"You're uncles? Twins, I presume."

"Yes. Twins. Two heroes, who left home and country in pursuit of something in a distant land. Looking for something better." He looked at Vig directly for a moment. "Quite the American dream, eh?"

Vig felt it was better to change the subject.

"What's the occasion?"

Ralph looked at him in surprise.

"The occasion? Ha! Of course, you are not an enthusiast. It is the Führer's birthday!"

Vig had been in some strange places before, and his natural curiosity wanted to see how this would play out. In this setting, Ralph seemed to stand differently, hold himself differently, even speak a little differently.

"This is an impressive setup, Mr. Engelstad, even for Vegas."

Ralph looked about the room proudly. "That which is meaningful to us is that with which we must take the most care, Herr Grün. Forgive me, I have other guests to greet. Look around, learn something, maybe you will be inspired."

He stepped away to a small group that had just come through the door behind Vig. No mention of the money, yet. No mention of Murray, yet.

Vig took a stein of beer from a tray held by one of the waitresses. Beside it was a bowl of what looked like large soft pretzels. They looked good, but he wasn't hungry. As always, the first beer didn't really touch the sides, it just dampened the sponge. He found the waitress, swapped his empty glass for a full one, and walked around to survey a few more artifacts.

There were a few busts and death masks… in fact one corner of the room seemed to be focused on this type of macabre. In another section there were weapons, mostly ceremonial swords and knives. A large collection of twenty or thirty Luftwaffe daggers displayed on a raised column seemed to be the centerpiece. A lot of the collection was paperwork – various papers previously owned by members of the army, navy, Luftwaffe and even a few from the SS.

So, this was what happened behind closed doors at the I.P. The first time Vig had met Ralph it was clear he was certainly not your normal casino owner. Vig had decided not to worry about why Ralph had asked him to come here and see how the night progressed.

"Herr Grün, I believe?"

He had been examining some medical records - and also rethinking the soft pretzels now that he was on his second beer - when the couple he had seen earlier stepped towards him.

"Vig is fine. Vig Green."

"Of course, Mister Green. Enjoying the ambiance?"

"It's certainly unique. Does Ralph throw this party every year?"

"He does, every year. It is the highlight of the calendar for him, and all of us in fact. Anyway, Mister Green, Herr Engelstad has something very special to show you."

He followed the couple through another set of double doors, into an office that seemed to be the same size of the conference room they had just left. What was unusual was that the double door came out at the back, behind the desk, in a nondescript side of the room. It was clear this door was not often used.

The office looked like it had existed for generations,

entirely separate and distinct from the property, and gave the impression that the hotel and casino had been built up around it. It was paneled floor to ceiling in dark brown wood, and around it hung what looked like replicas of old masters. The huge timber desk sat at one end. While it had a certain nineteen-thirties ambience, there was no hint of his other interests just one room away, Vig wondered was this his normal day-to-day office. Ralph was standing at the other end of the room and appeared to have just closed the door.

"Herr Grün! I hope you are enjoying the party, and the little mimeographed history lesson?"

"You clearly care about history. How did you get interested in this ... stuff?"

"This stuff? Herr Grün this is not just stuff that I got interested in. This is a legacy that I was born into."

He gestured for Vig to sit in the large leather chair in front of his desk. He walked silently to a globe-shaped drinks cabinet. It would have looked out of place anywhere but in this office. He took out three glasses and a bottle and set the glasses on the large leather-topped desk, then slowly poured three small drinks without adding ice or water. He picked up two of the glasses and handed one to Vig. He sat casually on the edge of his desk with the drink in his hand and shouted towards the door directly behind Vig. "Bringen ihn in jetzt!"

Vig didn't turn around, just took a sip of his drink. Brandy. He heard a door open behind him, and several pairs of feet walk in.

The two security guards from downstairs had come into the room, flanking a third person who shuffled between them.

Of course, it was Murray.

Ralph was clearly enjoying the moment. "Mister Wilson. Or is it Mister Wells? I am glad to see you are enjoying the party."

Murray did not seem all that surprised to see either of them. "Hey Vig. Long time no see."

"Hi Murray. It sure is."

Vig didn't know what this was all about, but he should have guessed that Murray would never have managed to actually tear himself away from Vegas, even if his life had depended on it.

"It turns out that we all know each other. Mister Green you have proven your level of trustworthiness, as have you Mister Wilson, but in rather a different way."

Murray spoke up. "Vig you fucker. You cut a bunch of blanks with my real goddamn name." He turned to Ralph. "This asshole conned me. The only reason you've gotten shit from…"

Ralph cut him off. "Yes yes, Murray. You took information given to you in trust and tried to steal from business associates of mine. You roped in another old associate of mine – Mister Green here – and tried to get him mixed up in your scheme."

Murray was incredulous or was faking it very well. "Ralph, buddy, this fucking guy wrote a hundred large in markers in my name and walked off with most of it. What did you net Vig? Sixty? Seventy grand? You piece of shit. You know what I've been through?"

Vig figured there was nothing he could add to proceedings, so he took another sip of his drink and said nothing.

Murray continued. "Wait. Old associate? You never said you knew him. What the fuck have you gotten me into?"

"Vig has not gotten you into anything, Murray." Engelstad was standing facing Murray by this point. He gestured to the chair. "Have a seat. Enjoy a drink."

Murray took the large empty chair beside Vig. Ralph turned to him and spoke. "What is it that you think you know about me, Murray?"

Before Murray could reply, Ralph continued. He stood over him, looking down at him, but seeming to stare right through him.

"I would wager that what you know, is wrong. I am not some trust fund child who invested his father's tyre money in a casino. My family came from a small village called Tashkend in a small district called Kovno-Wilnack. A very unspoiled and beautiful part of the world."

Murray glanced at Vig and looked like he was about to speak but something made him change his mind. Vig was making every effort to look cool and collected. Ralph continued, oblivious.

"Back in March 1917 the winter was cold. I mean, all the winters were cold, but this one was particularly cold with a thick layer of snow covering everywhere from horizon to horizon. However, family and love cannot be stopped by mere weather, and my grandmother was due to marry. It was a traditional wedding, with a large banquet planned at the bride's house, the bride being the only daughter in the family, and my great-grandmother and great-grandfather had spared no expense. The ceremony took place at a small church in Obstipoff, and my great-grand-parents had arranged for thirty sledges to take the bridal party from the church to the banquet."

He stood with his hands behind his back, looking out the window of his office eastward, toward Lake Mead.

"What a sight that must have been. Thirty sledges being driven across the snow, dogs barking and howling, all the guests wrapped up against the weather, smiling and laughing and excited for the night and for the future. It was that rarest of things in Russia at that time, a love match between a local boy and a local girl, a perfect match, and all the families in the parish and in the neighboring parishes had come out to celebrate. The party promised to be a long and memorable one."

A slight tremor had come into Ralph's voice.

"From what was reported after, the first sighting of wolves was made by the rearmost sledge when they were about halfway between the two towns. They signaled to the sledge in front of them, and the message was passed along. This was not a particularly uncommon occurrence at the time, but the wolves of course could be dangerous, especially when the snow was thick, and their normal prey was not plentiful."

"The second and third groups of wolves came from the front, forcing the leading sledges to stop, including that which was being driven by my great-grandfather. Who knows what would have happened had that first sledge not stopped but had tried to push through the line? I have asked that question, as I am sure that he did, many times."

"The killing and feeding went on for the rest of the evening, and on into the night. It was reported afterward as a battle, or a war, but it was neither. It was a bloodbath. One hundred and twenty wedding guests including the bridal party set off from Obstipoff. The only two who made it out of the snow were the bride and her father. My great-grandfather had ignored the plight of his own injured wife and walked through the snow to protect his only daughter."

"He knew that many would not understand his decision, how he could leave his own wife to the wolves, but he never regretted it. Of course, the local constable did not see it that way. My great-grandfather was hauled up in front of a magistrate to explain why he had survived and so many others had died. As if he… as if he would fear any kind of reprisal after watching his family die. He told the story with pride; his wife had made the sacrifice for her daughter, a sacrifice she had chosen, and that he had supported. He never let his daughter forget what was important; family, loyalty, sacrifice, and survival."

"Rather than the end, the night of death marked the rebirth of the family. It focused our heritage, our lineage, to two people. And from the blood of their family, strewn across the snow, came a purity of deed and thought that has lasted generations. This lesson she took with her and passed down to her own twin sons, and they took that lesson with them through their young lives. As they grew from boys to men, they witnessed first-hand their other mother - Russia - become a decedent den of corruption. There was no Soviet Union yet, but that would only make things worse, with layer upon layer of corrupt communist bullshit on top of a cesspit of graft and laziness and alcoholism. When they saw the Reich looking to the future, looking for a different way of living, they both left immediately for Germany, and joined the army."

Vig looked up. "So that's the paperwork I was looking at?"

Ralph didn't appear to hear him. "They enlisted, like many

others before and after, at the border. They fought shoulder to shoulder for four years in north Africa, the Sudetenland and Norway. It was in nineteen forty-four that they found themselves in a small town called Vilnius."

While he spoke, he stepped over to a large discolored map that hung on the office wall. It seemed to be a map of Europe but looked a few decades out of date. He stared at a spot, lost in thought.

"The Red Army marched against the glorious Wehrmacht in the summer of nineteen forty-four. The battle lasted nine days, and during those days the Reds encircled Vilnius, but the brave Rainer Joseph Karl August Stahl - despite being a mongrel with Finnish blood - lead three thousand brave German soldiers – including my uncle and father - out of Vilnius and back to the fatherland."

"What was to be Rainer Stahl's reward? Convicted in a kangaroo court of cleaning up Warsaw, and then seeing out his days breaking rocks in a filthy Russian gulag."

The last three words were hissed through gritted teeth.

"Was this a fitting end to a war hero, Herr Grün?"

Vig was clearly meant to say something. "What about your father and his brother?"

"My father and uncle? They stayed with him till the very end. He had saved three thousand soldiers' lives, including theirs. That was a debt impossible to repay. There are some in this world who understand the meaning of sacrifice, suffering, and respect. Do you know your own family history, Mister Green?"

"Three generations of – er – sporting involvement. Mostly ringside."

"Ah yes – pugilism. A very pure sport. Not just for the hand-to-hand, human element, but even from your perspective. The financial perspective. A certain purity to that side, too. A noble enough heritage. Irish, I presume?"

Vig nodded.

"Good people the Irish. Rejected imperialism to their credit. Never lost their identity, despite their recent moves towards the common market. Do you know why the German soccer team wear green when they play games outside their home pitch?"

Vig shook his head. He knew less about soccer than he did about the common market. This had taken a weird turn.

"They wear it because your countrymen were the first to come and play our countrymen after the zweite welt kriege. All in the past now, of course. However, the principles have not changed, the things that make us human have not changed. As for you Mr. Murray, do you know where you are from?"

Vig had almost forgotten Murray was still here. He just shrugged. "Poughkeepsie."

"No Murray, where are you from? We've been on this continent only a few generations, nobody is 'from' anywhere here... we are all the progeny of someone who was running away or running toward something."

"I guess, Polish. Probably about half Polish."

"Half Polish." He chuckled to himself. "Funny how I've never asked you that before."

Ralph walked back to the desk with the drink in his hand. He seemed to have forgotten he had poured one for Murray.

He sat down. "Now to business, Murray. There is a little lump of cash outstanding that brought you two together. Most of this was originally yours Mister Green, of which I understand Murray here took a large chunk for himself."

"That's bullshit Vig and you know it. I mean, that twenty grand was taken off me by a bookie. I didn't hand it over, I was shaken down for Christ's sake. You know this, Vig."

"You took that cash and attempted to hide it in a room in this very hotel, Murray."

Murray looked at him wide-eyed. Vig was pretty fucking wide-eyed himself but kept it on the inside.

"Twenty thousand dollars in cash is a large amount to steal from someone you hadn't met. But you had a room here and assumed you could stash that much behind the bedroom vent without it being found.

"You took it! You fucking took it."

"When known degenerate gamblers check in to my hotel under a false name paying the first few nights in cash, my staff know to keep a close eye on them."

"Fucking hell Ralph, I'm your friend." Murray was almost imploring.

The polite façade was slipping. "Fuck you Murray. You are nobodies' friend. You came as a guest to one of my parties – this very day last year in fact – and ingratiated yourself with me and my friends with your unfocused bigotry."

"What happened to the money?" Murray sounded like he was a little afraid of the answer.

Good question, Murray.

"The money was found by my staff and brought immediately to my office. My staff get well compensated for making finds like this from deadbeats. The deadbeats never complain, but I am surprised you never came looking for it? Although now that I think of it, your turning up anywhere looking for that much would have gotten around quick, and your friend Vig here might have heard. In fact, I'm quite sure that he would have."

"Right now, the money is sitting in the cage at the MGM. All the owner needs to do to get it, is to simply go to the cage and ask for it. It is not in my name, or either of yours, but the right name is all that's needed.

Vig spoke. "What's the big deal with this twenty grand? Why didn't you just... you know... keep it?"

"Oh, I did keep some of it. A single hundred-dollar bill. I soaked the bill in degreaser and discovered it was counterfeit. Probably a one dollar bill that has been reprinted. Is that true Mister Green?"

Vig lied. "I have no idea what you are talking about."

28 COUNTERFEIT

930 East Hanna Avenue, Indianapolis, Indiana
July 1979

Moving money around gave you an eye for good quality workmanship, and passing it off was part of the business, especially if you were left holding it unexpectantly. Vig never thought counterfeiting was a victimless crime, but he saw it no worse than point shaving in a basketball game or taking a fall in the ring.

The man on the right – Abbitt – spoke to Vig for the first time since he had arrived. "Is Richard even your real name?"

They were in the back of the print shop, in a small room next to the manager's office. There was one hundred thousand dollars sitting on a table, neatly stacked in two piles with five wrapped slabs per pile.

Vig answered. "No. It is not."

There was a pause. They were expecting Vig to tell them what it was. The man on the left – Brunson – eventually broke the silence. "Where are you going to mix this?"

"First, I'm going to test it. I'm going to pass it through my bag man, and another two handlers on the west coast. If any of them spot it, then they'll burn it. I'll get asked questions, but I'll deal with it. If it makes it to its destination, then the money will get fenced through a riverboat casino in St Louis. I have a team who will roll over the whole lot in a single weekend."

(Lying)

"A riverboat casino… isn't that a little risky?"

"I reckon there's a fifty-fifty chance that this money does not make it to St. Louis, but if it does, then it'll make it over the baize and back. When you run a game with six to five blackjack and three zeroes in roulette you don't need to hold it up to the light, you just stack it."

"This is the largest order we've ever filled. If you or any of your associates gets found holding this money, then we will have to be sure that there will be no link back to us."

"There is no link. You've spoken on the phone with our mutual acquaintance, who you trust enough. Our acquaintance has vouched for me completely, correct?"

"Correct."

"I do business based on trust. Also, I am taking the risk by travelling here, to you."

"Why did you insist on meeting us here, in the shop?"

"Well, I figured if you were willing to meet me here it meant that you were less likely to be operating a sting, or a wiretap. Handling counterfeit money is not going to get much time but passing it off or manufacturing it is. It is always better to meet counterfeiters in their factory, because that's the least likely place they will want the cops snooping around."

They looked at each other, Brunson smiled.

"Do we have a deal?"

"Fifteen thousand of mine for a hundred thousand of yours. We have a deal."

They shook on it, and Vig handed over the two overstuffed envelopes and began packing the 'money' into the small duffel bag he had brought for the purpose, while the other two men counted their slightly more legitimate cash. It was a lot to carry – real or fake – but holding cash was Vig's business.

"How are you going to get to St Louis with that?"

Vig has no intention of going to St Louis. He finished packing the bag and stood up.

"A pleasure meeting you. That's some fine work. We are unlikely to meet or speak again."

Vig walked out into the warm Indianapolis night. There was a taxi waiting around the corner on Bowman Avenue, out of sight of the front of the shop. He jogged over to it and – checking the roof sign matched the one he had stepped out of earlier – slid into the back seat.

"Airport?"

"Airport."

29 MISSOURI

3535 Las Vegas Boulevard South
April 20th 1980

"Are you saying you didn't know the money was counterfeit?" Ralph wasn't raising his voice, but he certainly sounded dubious.

"I don't move counterfeit money. You spend enough time around fighters and gamblers, you learn fast enough not to."

"Do you know where the rest of it is?"

Vig wished he knew. "I guess it is sitting baled in a warehouse in Mexico with the rest of the cartel millions. The guy who stole it from me was probably going to invest it in drugs, or pay off a drug habit, or be robbed by a drug dealer."

"Maybe. However, there is another eighty just like it – exactly like it - sitting in the MGM cage, reunited with its missing twenty. That's one hundred thousand dollars in counterfeit money currently sitting boxed in a Las Vegas casino cage. One could argue that it is the safest place for it, as long as Gaming don't show up with their brand new ultra-violet pens."

He chuckled again, seeing the look on Vig's face.

"A bookmaker came to me on the night of the big fight at Ceasers and asked for eighty thousand in MGM plaques. The floorman did not scrutinize the cash per the normal procedure,

146

so now has been forced into retirement. The eighty thousand was of course counterfeit, and when I saw Murray's counterfeit money that seemed to match, I figured I'd hold on to the whole lot and see if anyone came looking for it."

The pieces clicked into place in Vig's brain. Chuck had passed off eighty via some inside man into plaques and paid off some of his mobbed-up winners with the plaques before he left to keep the heat off. Finding Murray's twenty and chuck's eighty so close together must have really tickled Ralph's interest. He figured he'd play it cool. "I don't want the money back, if that's what you're asking."

"I presumed not. I presume you prefer the real thing. Well, the good news is that I have some work for you. Paying work. The fee is fifty thousand dollars… real dollars."

Murray piped up. "What's the work?"

Ralph ignored him, "It's a simple job. Collect the counterfeit money from the cage in the MGM. Deliver it to a location several hundred miles away and return here with a package."

Vig drained his glass. "I'm not interested in moving that amount of counterfeit money across a lot of state lines, and certainly not interested in moving whatever's in your 'package' without knowing what it is."

Ralph smiled. "I know you got this money in Missouri. It is poetic to me to think that Missouri is where the money is going to return. Retail value of that money is over thirty, but it could be acquired wholesale for a lot less – probably five or ten thousand. It's an appreciating asset. Every day the money isn't clocked it increases in value. And the fact that I have the whole batch means law enforcement are less likely to have seen it. In any case, this is not a favor I am asking, it is a job that I am offering. When you come back there will be another fifty thousand sitting in the same cage, but this time it will be real."

"When does this money have to move?"

"I'm not sure yet. September or October. I'll let you know. And Murray, in the meantime, keep your fucking mouth shut."

30 MIKE

One Royal Way
October 9th 1980

Kauffman Stadium was barely seven years old and still looked like something from the future. Purpose built baseball stadiums had become rare (the Royals and the Dodgers being the only real examples) and it felt to Vig like a different world. To him, sports was something done indoors, not out in the open. It would have been nice for them to be here to really enjoy the experience; the Yankees had come into town for game two of the AL Championship Series, but unfortunately while they were going to get to see a few innings, this trip was all business.

Vig and Gina stood out front of the stadium waiting to meet Vig's contact. They were supposed to be collecting two tickets for the game up behind the Water Spectacular but had been promised a short tour of the establishment by one of Ralph's friends. At seven fifteen - fifteen minutes late - a small door opened to the left of the right field turnstiles and a man stepped out and began walking towards them. "Victor, I presume?"

"Are you Buddy Long?"

"No, Buddy couldn't make the trip. I'm Mike Ferraro. And

who is this treasure?"

They all shook hands. "This is Gina. Pleased to meet you. I believe you have a couple of tickets for me?"

He laughed "Tickets? You don't know who I am?"

"I'm afraid not."

"I'm with the Yankees, part of the advance party making sure everything is ready for when the team arrives for the game later today."

Vig was confused. Mike saw his expression.

"Don't worry, you'll still get your tour, and you'll get to see the game. However, I have arranged for you to sit behind the Yankees dugout."

"Are we sitting with you?"

Mike smiled again. "No, you are not. I've made my own arrangements. Follow me."

They duly followed him back through the door. There didn't seem to be anyone else in the place apart from him and a few cleaners, still picking up after game one.

"If either of you are asked – and you won't be – the bag contains spare uniforms that we are getting the boys to sign for a charity auction."

He led them through the corridors until they got to the away team dressing room. The team uniforms were hanging side by side on the pegs, and fresh towels were stacked up beside the door. Vig looked at Gina. "Gina, could you take a walk down to the other dressing room?"

"Sure Vig." She knew it was for her protection. Mike watched her leave.

Once she was out of earshot, Mike gestured for the holdall. "Bag please?"

Vig shook his head. "This bag is for Buddy. Before I can hand it to anyone else, I need to make a call."

Mike didn't seem too surprised. "Sure thing. There's a phone right here outside the dressing room."

They stepped back outside, and sure enough there was a phone hanging from the wall outside the door, presumably the one used by reporters.

"Just lift the receiver. The ballpark has its own switchboard – give them the number and they'll put you through."

Vig did as he said. "Can you put me through to Nevada seven three one double-three double-one, please?"

"Sure thing caller. Do you have a specific recipient in mind?"

"Please ask for Mister Engelstad, and please tell his secretary that it is Mister Green calling."

"Sure thing caller."

Vig had to wait about a minute to be put through. Thankfully Ralph was always reachable in his suite, or the office, or on the floor if that was where he happened to be. While he waited, Mike just stood leaning against the opposite wall, staring at him, and occasionally glancing at the holdall.

Ralph was quick to answer. "Vig?"

"My contact didn't show."

"Yeah, he's sick."

Of course, he already knew. "There's a guy here claiming to be my new contact."

"Is he with you now?"

"Yep."

"Ask him what uniform the Brewers wore on their first game."

"What?"

"Just ask him."

Vig repeated the question to Mike, word for word.

Mike smiled. "You can tell Ralph that we wore Seattle Pilots uniforms with the logo ripped off."

"OK" said Ralph "The man in front of you is New York Yankees third base coach Mike Ferraro. You are about to help me bribe him to throw this game and lose his job. Oh yes, and he thinks the money is real." Ralph hung up the phone.

Mike smiled a big shit eating grin as Vig hung up.

"Bag, please?"

Vig handed it over. "Sorry I didn't recognize you. I'm not really a baseball guy."

"Huh – that's exactly what they said about me when I

played in the minors." He opened the bag and looked inside.

"What is this?" he scowled. All signs of congeniality had disappeared.

"Twenty. You get paid the rest after the game."

"Well, fuck you. Don't you trust me?"

"You are getting paid twenty grand plus another twenty for every runner you send home that gets called out up to a maximum of three, plus a bonus of twenty grand if the Yankees lose. The twenty in the bag is a show of good faith."

"Where's the rest? Does the skirt have it?"

"No. It will be available to you immediately after the game."

"This will be the last season, if not the last game, I coach for the Royals. If this goes the way I'm hoping they'll be baying for my blood up in the bleachers, so you better find a way to get me that slug quickly."

Vig nodded. "Give me your car keys. I'll put the money in the trunk and leave the keys under the wheel. I'll give you a hotel phone number you can call me at until midday tomorrow, in case there is a problem."

Mike looked dubiously at the bag. "Is that safe?"

Vig narrowed his eyes. "Unless you tell someone about it."

Mike seemed to think about this for a second, then relaxed. "Have you done this before?"

"Yes, I have."

31 BUZZING

They were awoken by the sound of the phone ringing; that low buzzing familiar to anyone who has stayed at the President Hotel. Vig picked up the receiver but didn't get an opportunity to say hello. It was Mike, and he was mad.

"Where's the fucking car? And where's the fucking money?"

"Calm down. What happened?"

"The car is gone. You are the only one who had a key. Where is it?"

"I don't know where the car is. We can't talk about this over the phone. Where are you?"

"Downstairs in the lobby of your hotel. If the front desk had given me your room number I'd be banging on your door right now."

Vig was relieved. "I'll be down in fifteen. And don't panic."

By the time he hung up the phone Gina was already in the shower. While she showered, he packed, carefully packing both of their things into the small overnight bag they shared. Then he showered himself, got dressed, and headed out to the

152

hallway, leaving Gina behind.

Even though it was eight floors, he took the stairs. On the ground floor there were two doors from the stairwell; one into a hallway leading to the lobby, and another heading to the kitchen from where he could leave by the back door, so this is where Vig headed. The kitchen was busy with the morning breakfast rush, so nobody paid any heed to Vig as he slipped by. It never hurt to be too careful. Once he left the kitchen by the delivery entrance, he turned left to walk around the side of the Ramada back towards the main door. He jogged up the steps, nodded to the doorman, and stepped into the lobby of the hotel he had just snuck out of.

Mike was standing at the concierge desk, with the phone sitting beside him – presumably that's where he had called Vig from. He was there on his own and there was no sign of the valet having started work yet; Vig figured he must have taken a cab to the hotel. At least that partially corroborated the "missing car" story. He walked softly through the busy lobby, keeping to the wall so that Mike wouldn't see him approach. Just as he came up behind him, the concierge looked up, but was savvy enough not to say anything, leaving Vig to announce his presence himself.

He practically whispered into Mike's ear. "Did you leave the keys where I said?"

Mike jumped out of his skin "Where the hell have you been?"

"Did you leave the keys where I said?"

Mike hesitated just a little too long.

"Yes of course. Under the wheel, just like you said."

"Which wheel?"

Again, a hesitation. Sigh.

"What does it matter which wheel? The keys, and the wheel, and the car, have fucking disappeared."

"Did you tell anyone else?"

Another hesitation. Seriously; fuck this guy.

"No way."

Vig knew exactly how to handle this type of asshole. He

didn't say anything else. Just stood there, casually looking Mike in the eye. Mike broke the silence.

"What now? I presume you have another way to pay me?"

"We need to find that money. Cars don't drive themselves away."

Mike was way too calm for a guy who had just been ripped off. Vig knew that leaving money in a car was surprisingly secure, especially at a ballgame where cars were not left overnight.

Vig stepped towards the front desk. "I'm just going to…"

Mike put his hand up to Vig's chest, as if to stop him. "Hold on. How do I know you didn't take it?"

Yep. Fuck this guy. Time for a change in approach.

"You don't know what I did. You don't know where the car is. You don't know who took it. You don't even know which wheel you put the key under. You don't know shit, apparently." Vig looked pointedly down at the hand at his chest. Mike removed it "So, what exactly do you want to do now?"

Vig already knew the answer. This asshole was going to keep acting as if he had been robbed and insist on getting made whole by Vig, by Gina, by Ralph, by anyone.

They were interrupted – right on cue – by Gina arriving in the lobby, looking none the worse for wear from the previous night. She had barely walked up and greeted them both when Mike headed off to make a call. Vig presumed he was going to call Ralph and claim that Vig had double-crossed him. She stepped closer to him, her voice low.

"All going to plan, Vig?"

"So far so good."

32 APRIL

28,000 feet
October 11th 1980

They hadn't been able to get a flight back to McCarran until the following morning. Ralph had convinced Mike to travel back with them to get paid 'again'. He sat across the aisle from Vig, with Gina sitting to his inside looking out the window.

Vig placed his hand on hers. She turned towards him and placed her other hand on his.

"Quite a trip, Vig."

It had been. They had checked into the hotel the night before the game, grabbed a little room service and hit the street early. Things should have been a little awkward between them, but with Gina things were never like that. She was always where she wanted to be; always in the moment. She hadn't hesitated when Vig had suggested she come along, the only thing that she insisted on was that they made the most of the trip to catch up and take in some bars the night before the game.

No problem, thought Vig.

'Some bars' turned out to be a gross understatement. They crawled from one end of Walnut Street to the other, and they didn't start out sober. The bars' clientele were hometown supporters mixed in with the usual Kansas City Friday night crowd. This is exactly the sort of crowd that they liked. Just like a Vegas crowd; there to have a good time in the company of people having a good time.

A lot had happened in the ten years between when Vig met Gina at Miss C-Gs and the reconciliation (of sorts) on the day of the Sugar Ray fight. Sixty percent of that that decade had been the happiest time of Vig's life, and the rest was just filler. Gina had asked him to deal a few private parties she held out in her place in Pahrump, as well as a few parties that she brought her girls into town for. She was always very clear with Vig that he was only there to deal, not to do any security or pour drinks. Gina was like that; she respected each professional's job and didn't assume anyone else's was harder or easier than hers.

Were they a couple? Vig never knew for sure, and to be honest he didn't pretend to know. After a time, he moved into a room in the Salt Wells Villa. It had been her idea. His apartment was being sold by the landlord, and he had been looking for a place to stay and run his small book from. She also gave him an old office with its own door at the back of the Villa. The office had a bed in it, as well as an old stove and a window overlooking the rear parking lot. Vig guessed that it had previously been used by a security guard or night worker.

Her only rule was a simple one; no bookmaking front of house, and no bookmaking with johns. That was fine by him. He was only taking mid-sized bets for visitors from LA and San Diego who knew how to reach him through old boxing contacts. A player would want to come to Nevada to place a bet outside the prying eyes of the strip casinos and their Federal reporting obligations. Very few of them were sharps, so he didn't really need to balance his action, he just had to stay the right side of the market. The only thing that he had to worry about was a boxing promoter with an injured fighter trying to get money on the other side and play a fix through his book, but his contacts from the city were still warm enough that he got fair warning of anything crooked. Mostly Vig used that information to keep his book balanced the old-fashioned way, by fading losing bets on a good line.

It was the ideal life for a while. Betting for a living. Living in a cathouse. Doing his socializing in the cathouse bar or on the strip with the madam. It really was close to a perfect life. Gina was also perfect. The way she handled the business, handled the girls, handled herself. Vig long ago stopped trying to put a label on their relationship. They vacationed together twice a year, had Christmas dinner together three times, and she even came back with him in one of his rare visits home in 1970 or 1971.

She didn't worry about things; she just did things. If she had a problem with a girl, she'd help the girl until it was time to stop helping and then just push her out. At that time, the main problem with girls was ensuring they kept away from hard drugs, it was the early seventies and there was a lot more than just recreational pot beginning to infiltrate the parties on the West Coast. When it did come time to put a girl out, she put a ticket in the girl's name at Bonneville Transit Centre, and either Vig or one of the security guys would give the girl a ride into town. Unfortunately, they almost never used the bus ticket, they just went straight back to work on the strip or in the hotel lobbies, turning enough on the first trick to pay for a room (or getting the john to pay for the night) then disappearing into the Strip the following night. Gina always – always – felt bad doing it, but she figured that if she treated the girls well, then the smart ones get their shit together and the dumb ones were beyond helping anyway.

It was one of those departing girls – April - that eventually put the wedge between Vig and Gina. It was nobody's fault what happened in the end, but it broke the trust between them for a very long time.

April had worked at the Villas for almost two years. She was a popular girl with the regulars, a solid seven out front but apparently a nine when at work. "Full GFE" as they would say nowadays, provided she was treated well. It's not that she loved the life, but she seemed to thrive outside of work. She had hobbies, and interests, and a family that she visited. She saved a little money and had plans to travel for as long as her looks would carry her. Not exactly the 'hooker with the heart of gold' but certainly the 'hooker without the usual brain of mahogany'.

She had plans to move east to work with her sister in a strip club in Atlantic City, and then work her way up to New York or jump the puddle to Europe. The weekend that she was planning to leave, Gina was out of town for the weekend, but they had said their farewells and Gina had wished April well. Vig was due to drive her to Vegas, where she had planned to stay overnight and catch the morning flight east to start her new life.

They were due to leave the Villas at lunchtime on Saturday. Vig had been finishing up some bookkeeping in his office, when his phone rang (Gina had a private line installed so he could run his business without taking up the Villa's own line). It was a voice he recognized.

"Arlo. It's Saturday? What's the occasion? Is there a college ball game I forgot was on?"

"Hey Vig. Glad I caught you. How are you doing?"

"We're square so it's all good." (he laughed) "Nothing to report. What can I do for you?"

"Me and a buddy of mine are heading down to Vegas tonight, for a long weekend. We are looking for some professional female company, and seeing as you..."

"Come on Arlo, you know the drill. Call Gina at the main office, she can make a date for you guys here or in town. I'm not in the cat business."

"You live there, dude! You aren't just in the business; you are IN the business. We don't want some agency girl; we want something a little special come stay with us for the weekend."

Arlo and Vig were not exactly friends, but they had worked a lot of fights together in the early days, and Arlo usually looked Vig up when he came to town to see a big-ticket card.

He had visited the Villas before as a client and had – Vig had checked – been a perfectly respectable customer.

Before Vig could respond, there was a knock on his office door. It was April.

"Hi Vig, ready when you are. I tossed my bag in your car. You shouldn't leave the trunk unlocked like that."

"I'll just be a minute." He paused and covered the receiver with his hand. "Wait. What are your plans for tonight?"

"Stay in town, take in a show…"

"Seriously? You going to do any lobby-surfing?"

"I might try and pick up an extra fifty for tips." She winked.

"I've got a friend coming to town, from LA. You want me to introduce you? He's looking for your kind of company."

She looked dubious. "You know this guy long? Gina wouldn't appreciate me taking a contact off the books."

"You're off the books now, remember? What do you think?"

"He a boxer?"

"He was. Still in shape, at least the last time I saw him."

"OK then, let's pull up to meet him and say hi. Hang out with us until either I decide to bail or decide to stay."

"Deal. Wait in the car and I'll be right with you."

So that was two birds with one stone. Vig could drop off April with Arlo, and both would get what they want. Arlo would drop a ton of money on her for the night, and she'd get the sendoff she needs without getting hassled by doormen on Freemont street. Everybody wins.

The spin into town was uneventful, small talk, a little talk about her travel plans. They were due to meet Arlo at the Treasure Island valet stand. As they pulled in, Vig could see that Arlo was there with his friend, a short Latino guy, possibly another boxer or former boxer. April didn't wait till the car stopped… she just rolled the window down and said hi.

Both the guys smiled and said 'hi' back. Arlo reached out to shake her hand through the window. She looked at Vig and winked. "You can drop me off here Vig, I'll call you from Paris!"

She stepped out and immediately the short Latino guy began talking to her, already clearly enamored. Arlo walked around the car and leaned in the drivers-side window. "Thanks Vig, she seems really sweet. You going to pick her up on Monday or something?"

"No Arlo, she leaves town tomorrow. She'll hang with you for a few hours. A hundred till midnight will cover you. That's more than she'll ask for, but fair is fair."

He took out his wallet.

"Jesus Christ, Arlo. Put that shit away. I'm just dropping a friend off."

Vig stuck his head out of the window. April was leaning on the shoulder of the short Latino, and they were both smiling. "You OK April?"

"Never better, Vig!"

She never made her flight to Paris.

It's not that Gina blamed Vig for April's death, it was more that he'd blurred the line between his business and hers and this had upset the rest of her girls. She believed that she had let April down, had not protected her. Plenty of her walk-offs had ended up in bad cathouses, drug situations, or worse. The difference was they hadn't been given a ride there by the house.

Vig tried hard to find out what happened, but of course the story was the same. It turned out that Arlo and Short Latino didn't know each other that well, they had headed off with April and bumped into a few mutual acquaintances and partied together into the night. Arlo found himself somewhere without them and figured they'd done their own thing. Short Latino's story was the same, that they weren't acquaintances, just some guys that recognized him from a fight in LA; they had become separated somewhere between clubs and he assumed that April was doing her thing with "those other guys". All very ambiguous, but all very Vegas.

April had been found in a hotel room booked in her own name at the Flamingo, full of Quaaludes and barbiturates and scotch and stone dead.

Vig spent a few months trying to track down the rest of the guys, but with no luck. Arlo was no help as he had his own parole issues which meant he kept his head down. Hooker dead. No suspects. The end.

Gina was sad rather than mad. Nothing was said, but Vig knew that he had to move out of the Villas.

If only for appearances sake, they kept up some semblance of whatever they had, but eventually it just petered out, until Vig realized one day that it had been three weeks since they had last spoken. Then three months passed, then three years. And then the Sugar Ray fight happened, and then it was now.

33 RALPH

McCarron Airport Arrivals
October 11th 1980

They had not made a clear arrangement with Ralph at the other end of the flight. Vig figured that he would either meet them there himself or send a car. McCarron was quieter than normal, and there was no limo driver to be seen at the meet-n-greet.

Vig wasn't going to fuck around with Mike and was definitely not going to give him a chance to change his mind. With no bags to collect the three of them headed straight out to the concourse and hailed a cab. Mike pulled open the front passenger door and sat in. He had said very little in the air, and Vig was happy for that to continue on the ground.

Vig reckoned Gina had better places to be than where they were going. "You want to head back to your place Gina?"

She shook her head and without saying a word slid beside him in the rear seat of the taxi.

"Imperial Palace please. Valet stand."

They sat in silence as they had on the plane, until the cab made its way into town pulled up at the I.P. Mike jumped out without a word to light up a cigarette. Vig paused for a moment and then handed the driver a twenty and quietly told him to stay close until the twenty ran out. He figured if either of them wanted to make a quick getaway they would know in the first few minutes. Ralph was right there in the lobby waiting for them, a big smile on his face.

"Mike! Sorry to hear about the robbery. Come for a drink and tell me what happened."

Mike looked blankly at him for a second, then checked himself and smiled back. "Hey Ralph." And then quieter "You think this place is a little conspicuous? I'm a figure of hate back home now and this morning's papers won't help none."

"Don't sweat that. You are here as my guest as you have been before, just taking in the tables to blow off a little steam, right?"

"Sure thing Ralph. Although the funny thing is, I think I'm going to do well this trip."

Ralph laughed, but there was an edge to it. "You do better than most people every time you come down here."

By this time the four of them had walked through to the bar in the center of the casino floor and taken a small raised table. Ralph took one of the four seats and gestured to the others to sit down. Once they were all seated, he spoke.

"Vig tells me your car was stolen, cash and all?"

"Yep. I told him that the car was a dumb place for the…"

A flicker of something on Ralph's face, and his tone shifted dramatically. "I don't want you to fucking blame Vig. He knows how to handle money and knows that cars just don't get stolen from ballpark lots. Do you want to know how I've been spending my morning?"

Mike looked from Vig to Ralph, then nodded. "Sure."

"I've been calling every police station and impound lot within three hours of the car park. No sign of your car. Not abandoned, burned out, or anything."

"Whoever boosted it would have found the cash and made a break for it. It's probably over a border by now."

"Perhaps." Ralph looked like he was sure it was anything but the case.

Mike was nonchalant "So.. what now? I need to get paid.

My career on third is probably over, if not now then by the end of the season."

Their drinks arrived; four beers. There was a brief break in the conversation. Ralph picked his drink up and took a long draught.

"Mike. I brought you here to explain to you personally what is going to happen."

Another mouthful of beer.

"You paid someone to move the car. That person double crossed you. Or maybe they are lying low until things blow over. Either way it doesn't matter to me."

Mike was incandescent.

"Fuck you Ralph. You don't know what you are talking about. Have you been listening to this guy?" He nodded towards Vig. "Ralph, really? You think I'd rip you off?"

"I think if you would send that runner home, you are capable of anything."

"I didn't take that money."

The waiter stepped over with four more beers. Ralph's first was empty, Gina's and Vig's were about half full, Mike's was untouched.

Ralph was talking mostly to himself at this point "I wonder how you find someone to steal a car at such short notice? I'm guessing you went to a local bar – maybe the Silverleaf – and gave some shitheel who wasn't too drunk a twenty-dollar bill to put your car in a parking garage. You were probably smart enough to pick an out-of-towner who was less likely to recognize you."

Mike opened his mouth, but nothing came out.

Ralph laughed. "You sports guys are so fucking predictable."

While he had been talking, the waiter had pulled another chair up to the table. Murray appeared and sat down at the table smiling from ear-to-ear.

"Ralph! And Vig and Gina! How you guys doing?"

The effect was dramatic. Mike went white. Vig had known that this bit of theatrics was part of the plan, but he was not aware that Ralph had used Murray. Ralph was a little smarter – or a lot dumber - than Vig had given him credit for. He broke the silence.

"Don't make a move Mike. Just stay right where you are. There was a time when trying to rip off a hotel owner in Vegas would have ended very badly for you. But you're a public guy with connections of your own, so I will keep this very simple. The owner Stienbrenner already wants you gone; he has already embarrassed himself by being caught cussing up a storm on live TV. The only thing is, the manager has already told Stienbrenner to go fuck himself. Dick Howser has said a lot of things over the years but has not until now taken an opportunity to tell his boss to go fuck himself."

"What's going to happen? Is he going to fire me?"

"Nobody here knows or gives a fuck if he's going to fire you. Or have you killed. Or burn your house down. What I DO give a fuck about is helping my buddy get the team and the manager he wants. The team is the Royals, and the manager is Dick Howser. But Howser won't quit or he forfeits some sort of signing bonus, so he has to be fired."

"Dick stuck up for me?"

Ralph leaned back and laughed out loud.

"Dick stood up for Dick, you idiot. You are just a pawn here. The only reason I sent Murray to take the money off you is because I needed to be sure that Dick would get fired before I'd leave you with the payoff. If I decided to withhold, I didn't want you to be sore about it."

Mike was indignant. "You sneaky fuck."

"Don't speak so soon you sneakier fuck. You are here to steal from me. The good news is that Murray is here with your money."

"The money?"

"Every penny. While I'm sure Murray has poked around in the bag a little…" Murray looked hurt but didn't say anything "…I'm pretty sure he hasn't stolen too much of it."

34 SUNRISE

3595 S Las Vegas Boulevard
November 21st, 1980 (7.06am)

Vig had had many breakfasts in this exact spot since he
had first come here with Gina in 1969. Some had been
business, and some had been pleasure. In that time, it
had become one of the most recognizable places this end of
the strip, with a unique style that would last over three decades
until the place was renamed Bills, and then was renovated and
again renamed the more modern Cromwell.

Vig and Gina were back in town after spending just over a
month away. After the trip to Kansas City - and the shit with
Ralph and Murray - they had done something unfamiliar to
both of them; they had taken a vacation. They had first
travelled to see Gina's family in Minnesota, gone to Tijuana in
Baja to party, and returned to Vegas to take care of a little
unfinished business. The next stop was going to be New
Orleans to see the Sugar Ray Leonard and Roberto Duran
rematch. Life was good, but with Gina, Vig could never escape
the feeling that the unexpected was just around the corner.

The business they had to attend to was simple. Gina had
promoted one of the working girls to run the Villas, a girl who
had been with her from the start, and who had moved from

the cathouse to the restaurant when it was clear she had skills as opposed to just 'skills'.

Vig had some money to collect, mostly some closed out accounts with other bookies, but they had one big lump waiting for them in the MGM; they were going to finally collect from Ralph.

In the end, Ralph had paid off the third base coach in cash and hotel credit at the I.P., and the guy had done what every other degenerate does in that situation, he'd checked in and gambled the lot, chalking up some markers of his own to boot. That's why Ralph had brought him to Vegas, to get the payoff back and get the balance back in his favor. Murray had been paid off too. He'd offered to take the counterfeit money off Ralphs hands for pennies on the dollar, but Ralph knew better than to have Murray walking around with that incriminating slug more than he had to. He began using Murray as a bag man for a lot of his business, which surprised Vig but suited him just fine as it meant he could keep away from both of them. He didn't have any politics back then, but swastikas were swastikas whatever the decade.

Gina and Vig had been paid for their little part in the caper, but of course there were complications. Ralph wanted to pay them back in bills that were out-of-state and uncirculated as the authorities were sniffing around him and his casinos at the time (it would be another five years before his birthday parties for Hitler would become public knowledge). The hundred grand they had been promised had had another fifty added, and was not being paid from the cage, but was being handed over in cash in a room on the twelfth floor of the MGM, right across the street from where they were eating breakfast. They had asked Ralph who was making the handover and his response was 'not to worry about it', so Vig had guessed Murray would be involved in some way, and that naturally concerned him.

They ate quietly, taking their time, talking in hushed voices.

Both wanting for their own reason to get the collection over with. Gina had hinted that returning to live in Las Vegas was optional, and that she might sell up her business. Vig himself was tiring of the pace, and the heat, and wanted to make a change. They had both hinted to each other that they might stay in New Orleans after the fight. Two hundred and fifty grand could go a long way in Louisiana in 1980.

It had just past seven when Vig heard the first sirens. They were not uncommon on the strip, but when more alarms and sirens joined the cacophony it was clear something out of the ordinary was happening outside

Vig put a twenty onto the table and stood up to go. Gina – sensing something was wrong – stood up with him and without exchanging a word they just headed for the side door that led out to the road opposite the MGM. Traffic had stopped, and there was a smell of smoke in the air, it was hard to see exactly where the smoke was coming from, but it seemed to be thickest above the MGM lobby right across the street. A police cordon had formed, and they were struggling to keep people back, as the MGMs guests were pouring out of the front door onto the strip, some were also emerging from the car park entrance directly across from where Vig and Gina were standing.

"Jesus Christ, Vig."

He didn't get a chance to respond. The front door of the MGM was blown open by a huge deafening fireball that spilled out onto the strip. Vig couldn't tell if anyone was killed or injured, but it was clear that people had been clearing out of the lobby and gaming floor right when the explosion happened. The police had struggled to keep people away but after the explosion people kept plenty back themselves.

They stood there rooted to the spot, watching with the rest of the crowd as the MGM burned and the cloud of dust made it across the street, covering the assembled crowd and somehow muffling the sounds from the sirens and wounded. There didn't seem like anything they could do. They just stood there, hand in hand, watching the fire tenders working and the crowd getting bigger from the remaining refugees from the hotel and the inevitable onlookers.

It was only after the fire was under control that the enormity of the situation become clear. There had been ambulances ferrying people from the scene to Sunrise Hospital most of the morning. Apart from those physically affected, thousands upon thousands of MGM guests were just standing there, not knowing what to do. The neighboring hotels had set up tables and chairs and were giving out water and coffee to all those who wanted it. Some were still in their dressing gowns and pajamas, and some in evening wear, it was a bizarre scene.

Gina quietly reminded Vig that there was one very important person who was in the hotel, and they had no idea where he was or even if he was dead or alive.

"This is an awful situation, but somewhere in there is a man with a bag of money for us, and the longer this goes on the more likely it becomes we never see it again."

Vig knew that she was right. Gina suggested that they go to the hospital. If Murray was alive, he would go to ground. If Murray was hurt or worse, the hospital would know. One of the incredible things about Las Vegas was that something as huge as the MGM burning down affected the surrounding quarter block, but beyond that, the reels and wheels were still spinning. They had to walk halfway up the strip before they could get a cab – traffic was hell in both directions – but eventually managed to flag one down who had just dropped off someone at the back of the Flamingo

The cab driver took it all in his stride; "Quite a show, eh?" but Vig and Gina were in no mood to talk. They arrived at the hospital a little after nine. A small crowd had formed, and ambulances were still arriving. There was a harried looking clerk out front answering questions from worried friends and relatives, and Gina made a beeline for him.

"Stay back Vig, I got this."

"What are you talking about Gina?"

"Trust me."

She pushed her way to the front of the crowd.

"Name please ma'am." The clerk barely looked at her.

"Mine or my husbands?"

He looked up. "Your husbands."

"Murray Wilson."

"Do you know if he was in the building?"

"Yes, he was taking a nap in his room."

"And you are?"

"Mrs. Gina Wilson, his wife."

"What room number?"

"I'm sorry, I don't know. I was coming to meet him at the MGM. Can you please tell me if he is okay?"

He looked at his list. "I'm afraid I don't have any information on your husband, ma'am. The hospital has set up a room for relatives, if you'd like to wait there, we can bring you news when we have it."

"I'll check back later."

Gina stepped back to where Vig was standing, just about within earshot, but out of the clerk's eye line.

"Well, he isn't here, unless he's given a false name."

Vig looked thoughtful for a moment. "I have an idea."

He walked over to the clerk, approaching from the side.

"Hi there. I'm looking for my brother, Marcus Wells. He was staying in the MGM."

The clerk checked the list. As he moved down the list with his pencil, he stopped abruptly.

"Sir, can you go and speak to the registrar at hospital reception, please?"

"Come on, just tell me if my brother is here?"

He looked me in the eye. "He is listed as being checked in to the hospital earlier today, I'm afraid I cannot tell you any more than that."

"OK, thanks buddy."

The line at reception was shorter, and they kept the line short with a security guard directing new arrivals outside to the clerk like a triage for relatives. The receptionist was a young woman, and she informed Vig that 'Marcus' has arrived about thirty minutes beforehand suffering from smoke inhalation but was now stable. Vig was surprised when she gave up his room and bed number and told him he could visit, as long as he didn't stay too long. It was very casual, for what was basically a field hospital serving a disaster zone.

Vig and Gina made their way to where Murray was, not sure what to expect. There was a room with a hastily drawn sign saying 'smoke inhalation - m' pasted to it, and that was where he apparently was. Vig wondered what the 'm' stood for; MGM? mild? male? They opened the door to find a room with about a dozen beds in it, most of which were filled, some of the occupants wearing masks.

Vig looked along the row of beds, not sure exactly sure how or if he would recognize Murray, but he needn't have worried. The familiar figure of Murray was visible in the furthest bed, facing the door, motionless. Vig gestured to Gina and they made their way quietly towards the foot of his bed.

He was asleep, fast asleep. He didn't look the worse for wear at all, just looked his usual slightly disheveled self, still clothed in the light khaki suit he always wore. However there was something even more surprising; Murray was clutching a duffel bag between both arms. Vig looked at Gina and back to the bag. She hadn't taken her eyes off it. He could hear her softly breathing despite the noise of the oxygen machines dotted around the room.

"We're doing it, Vig."

"Gina, we have to be careful."

"It's our money, honey. Keep watch."

Before he could object, she reached over and gently unclasped Murray's hands from the bag, lifting it gingerly off the bed. He stayed asleep the entire time. The bag was heavy, money heavy. She turned back towards Vig, kissed him gently on the cheek, and headed towards the door. Vig paused to look at the sleeping figure in the bed for one final time, then turned and followed her.

35 DOKA

Route 107, Tambor De Alajuela
August 1985
(Five years later)

Crossing the river Poás northbound always felt like leaving 'modern' Costa Rica and heading to a more pastoral past. Vig had driven this route a few times before, up to see the smoldering volcano at Poás, and feed the chipmunks. You walk up the hill through the forest, and by the time you get to the top steeped in sweat the goddamn mist has closed in so you can't see anything. You find yourself standing on the edge hoping for an eruption to justify the walk.

Gina was at the wheel of a car that was about as old as the volcano itself. Driving without air conditioning in Costa Rica in August was no picnic. They had the windows down and the radio blaring. Then, as now, all Tico music sounded the same to Vig. She had told him that they were heading to a coffee plantation called Doka.

"Mind if I smoke, Vig?"

"That's new."

"Not that new. I smoked from age fifteen to about twenty-five, and just started again about three weeks ago."

Vig smiled. "So how long did you quit for?"

She tapped her ash out the open window. "Fuck you Vig. You just go ahead and remember I'm twenty-nine now and forever."

Vig laughed. "What's the plan here? How do you even know this guy still has our money?"

"He's gone native in the last five years. Married and divorced a local, invested in a couple of fishing boats and other businesses, including the coffee plantation we're headed to."

He was apprehensive about just showing up at this guy's door and seeing if it was really Chuck. Gina didn't seem worried. Vig didn't know what else she knew but he trusted her enough not to ask for details.

They drove for another thirty minutes, and eventually arrived at a large gate like many others they had passed. This one had a small 'D' in wrought iron, so Vig guessed it was the Doka estate. There was a small button and speaker hanging to the right of the gate. Gina pulled the car over to the side of the road and shut off the engine.

They got out, hit the button, and waited. After a few minutes, there was a crackling sound and a voice said 'Buenas, Que."

Gina pressed the button and to Vig's surprise said, "This is Victor Green and Gina Wilson".

There was silence on the other end, and after a few minutes the voice returned and said carefully in English "Someone will be down shortly."

Gina leaned back on the hood of the car, lit another cigarette, and stared at Vig with a wry smile on her lips.

"Any idea what happens now?"

They waited for a while at the gate, Vig began to think nobody was coming. Gina had gone through the rest of her cigarettes; she seemed relieved by the time she had finished the last one. Just as she stubbed it out, they heard a new noise in the distance; the sound of wheels on gravel. A middle-aged woman was walking down towards the gate, carefully pushing a wheelchair ahead of her. She was not dressed for the weather, wearing what looked like a fine dressing gown or house coat draped over her shoulders. Her hair was mostly grey and pulled back in a tight bun behind her head. The figure in the chair was a frail looking man, sitting upright and alert despite the chair.

Gina stood beside Vig. "Recognize him?"

He wasn't sure what she was talking about at first, but as the figure came closer, he began to look familiar. The build was completely different; half the weight he had been when he had last seen him. But it was unmistakably Chuck the bookie. He had changed a lot in the years since they had last seen him at the Other Place, drinking coffee.

As he approached the gate, he addressed the woman pushing the chair without taking his eyes off Vig and Gina. The voice hadn't changed much.

"Elaine my dear. I'd like to introduce you to two people whose names will be familiar, but you assuredly have not met. This is Victor Green and Gina Wilson. The original Victor Green and Gina Wilson."

The original? The woman – Elaine – had walked towards the gate and was unlocking it. "Welcome to Doka."

They walked back up the track behind Chuck and Elaine, in silence. The plantations spread out from the track in both directions, uniform fields of tall green coffee plants. Vig wondered why they had come down themselves; presumably in a plantation of this size there were staff who could be sent down to open the gate? Maybe Chuck had decided that he wanted to see the two of them for himself.

Vig had imagined many times what he would do if he met Chuck again. He wasn't much of a shouter or a fighter, but he did know how to exact revenge one way or another. What he mostly felt now was curiosity; what the fuck had happened to this guy?

As the path wound its way through the coffee fields a large building came into view. It was a low-sling wooden house. This was no plantation shack, it was a beautiful house with a wide porch out front, with a large dining table surrounded on all but one end with seats. There was a small ramp beside the steps up to the porch – presumably for the wheelchair – and Elaine pushed Chuck up the ramp and tucked him into the end of the table.

He sat without saying anything. Elaine was beside him.

"Elaine – some coffee please."

Elaine stepped into the house, with a final protective look back at Chuck, who remained almost motionless.

Gina beckoned Vig to sit down. They took a chair beside each other on the house side of the table, facing out over the plantation. There were two electric fans over the porch which – along with the breeze – tried to keep the mid-afternoon heat at bay.

When they sat, at last Chuck spoke.

"What do you think of the plantation, Vig?"

He didn't wait for an answer.

"These are believed by many to be the best coffee trees in Costa Rica. I purchased it from the Vargas family about a year after we last spoke. They had called the coffee 'Three Generations'; but they asked me not to continue to use the name as it represented their families' commitment to the coffee for most of this century. I think they hope to buy the place back some day." His laugh turned into a cough which went on for a minute. It was clear he was not a well man.

It was Gina who spoke.

"You bought this with Victor's money?"

"Not exactly."

Elaine came back outside, carrying a tray with a tall ceramic coffee pot and four gold-rimmed porcelain cups. No sugar or milk, of course.

"Tell them the whole story, Charles."

36 CHARLES

Doka Coffee Plantation
August 1985

Chuck – Charles – had quite a story. Having taken Vig and Gina's money after the fight, he had fled south to Nicaragua by plane with his sister Elaine, and then to Costa Rica over land.

He had known for some time he was sick and had been planning to retire as soon as he had accumulated a sufficient retirement fund. When Vig and Gina showed up at the Other Place, he had seized the opportunity to accelerate his retirement plans and abscond.

Elaine had been a nurse in Seattle, and was running from a failed marriage, so she was happy to come with him to work as his carer and companion. The money he took was partially to pay her to live with and care for him until the end came. He had hoped to find something to invest in that would provide an income for them, and also retain some capital value for Elaine after he died. Most importantly, the investment opportunity had to be discreet. He had done his research and decided that Costa Rica had the right combination of discretion, but rule of law, that meant he could be sure that he would not be too badly ripped off.

He had gotten lucky right off the bat: within a few months of arriving he had heard about Doka, and just walked up to the gate and offered the Vargas' family his entire retirement fund to take the plantation off their hands. They had taken a little time to consider it, but had accepted the offer with little negotiation, they had asked that all of the staff would be kept on for at least one more season. Charles was smart. He told them he'd keep all the staff on for a year and keep the foreman for two years at least. That sealed the deal.

To avoid being followed from Las Vegas – he owed other people money of course - he bought the plantation under a false name. He signed the deed, moved into the house with Elaine, and waited to die. With the same foreman in place, and the same staff (many related to the Vargas family) the plantation didn't change much despite changing hands. Charles and Elaine spent their time in the house and the coffee grew up and was cut down, season after season, as it had been for many decades.

There were few visitors to the plantation, other than a doctor who came in from San Jose once a month to check on Charles. They rarely left Doka, and if they did it was to head for either the Pacific or Atlantic beaches, both being within a couple of hours drive. Charles would sit and read while Elaine would spend her time enjoying the year-round warm clear sea.

To Charles' surprise and delight, the coffee business went from strength to strength, and he found himself becoming unexpectedly wealthy. In the absence of anything else to do, he invested in upgrading the plantation's equipment and facilities, as well as investing in a pension fund for the staff. The surplus was set aside as a nest egg for his sister.

"I always figured you would track me down. I actually thought it would happen sooner, to be honest."

The group had retired to the main living room in the house. Charles was seated in a large leather chair, and the rest of the party were sitting in large sofas around a coffee-table, sharing – of course – a pot of coffee.

"How do you think anyone would find you here?" Vig looked at Gina. "How DID you find him?"

Gina smiled and looked at Charles, and he smiled back.

Vig had a flashback to the moment in the bar when he had suspected the two were in cahoots. "What the fuck is going on here?"

Gina took a sip of her coffee and sat back. "He bought the place in your name, Vig."

"Miss Wilson is right, Victor. I couldn't put this place in my own name due to my debt and – ahem - legal problems, so the obvious thing to do was put it in yours. I figured by the time you tracked me down through property registry or a private eye or something, I would be either dead or would have found a way to pay you back."

Gina was still smiling. Vig didn't understand why.

"I have your money if you want it, Victor. When the bank opens tomorrow, you could take it and leave. In your shoes, it's exactly what I would do. They would stay here for the remaining short years and figure out how to transfer Doka to Elaine somehow. However, there is another option. I have enough put aside to set us up back home in the US. At this point, I don't care if any of my other pursuers find me, and I cannot imagine they are still looking. You could just take the plantation rather than the cash. No paperwork needed. It is already yours and Gina's."

Vig was speechless. Luckily Gina wasn't.

"You said you'd pay us back Chuck, and you did. We'll take it. Take your time moving out, as someone will have to teach us how the fuck you grow coffee."

37 COFFEE

Doka
September 1985

The coffee business is simple if you have good people working for you, the right climate, and a large enough plot of land. A good foreman will ensure that the beans are picked at the right time, and you need the right people and machinery to do the washing and milling. You also needed time; the coffee was planted about five years before it was harvested.

Doka was a little different to other Costa Rican coffee plantations; the family believed that the bean should not be heated at all before it was roasted, so they didn't polish their beans. Also, for a long time they had being taking in two harvests a year; one in Spring and one before Christmas. This two-harvest schedule meant that you could keep most of the staff on-site for almost the entire year.

Vig gave notice on his small apartment in San Jose and gave notice in person to Ronald Sacco that he was not coming back to work. Initially Sacco didn't take it too well, until Vig reassured him that he would hand over all his whales and prospects to one of the other staff. In the end Sacco's only worry had been that Vig might take some of the bigger leads with him. When Vig told him that he was getting into the coffee business, Sacco was at once relieved but also amused.

"Those fucking guys will rob you blind, Vig. Good luck."

He meant it.

There had been nothing to sign – Charlie just showed them the deed and contract with Vig's name on it. The timing was good. Gina and Vig had a couple of months before the 'little harvest' in November to get their heads around the coffee business. Charles and Elaine moved into the foreman's wing of the house because it was downstairs, so Vig and Gina just took over the rooms in the top floor. Beside the main bedroom upstairs there was also a room where the files and records for the business were kept in a large office dominated by a large dark wooden desk.

Vig spent time getting to know the land, the people and the machinery, while Gina focused on the books and the suppliers, truckers, jute bag manufacturer and others that they needed to keep the coffee beans flowing. The staff didn't seem overly concerned about the fact that another two people had moved in with the 'boss' and seemed to be taking over. They were well paid year-round and well looked after, so they figured they would either be worse off and leave, or better off and stay, or nothing would change.

When Gina worked on the books she would sit in the upstairs office. She worked out a simple system with her three colleagues; if the radio was on, she could be disturbed, if it was off, then she did not want to be interrupted. Vig tried not to bug her so when he wasn't down in the washhouse or in the clearings where the drying happened, he would sit in the house or on the porch, either alone or talking to Charles or Elaine who were always around.

While at first it was weird for Vig and Gina to be living with a brother and sister around all the time, as the weeks went by it became comforting to know they were there in case they needed any help. The foreman - José - spoke perfect English, but Charles was encouraging Vig and Gina to learn Spanish, so when the foreman came to meet them, he spoke in the local tongue and Vig would ask Charles to clarify the bits he didn't understand. Vig was a quick learner, and by the time the first berry was picked in mid-November he was asking less and less.

In the evenings the four of them would sit with José and play rummy on the porch or in the living room depending on the weather. It was funny for Vig to be doing things with Gina like this, as most of the time they had spent together over the years had been spent alone, i.e. just the two of them. Of course, Gina was at ease in every situation she found herself in.

That winter the little harvest looked like it was going to be bigger than planned, so José put out the word to the workforce that they would need two or three extra pickers to get the good quality cherries in before the end of the year. Vig took it as a positive omen that the first harvest would be a good one, and told him to hire whoever he needed to make it so.

A week or so later he told Vig that he had found two workers willing to come on for eight weeks casual picking work; one of the existing workers' cousins, and his companion. They had worked in coffee plantations in Colombia and Argentina in the past, so seemed ideal. What Vig didn't realize at the time is that these two would bring down a whole heap of trouble on Doka.

38 TELEBETTING

There is a big gap between Vig and Gina being chased onto the roof by Sacco's henchmen and Vig ending up working for him in a bookie's call center in Costa Rica six years later. Both men turned out to be a lot more pragmatic in the end. It doesn't pay too much to bear grudges or have enemies in their business, especially with enemies with a long reach like Sacco.

After the MGM fire, Vig and Gina stayed together / not-together for over a year working through some of the money. They both went quietly back to work; both keeping a lower than usual profile and mostly staying away from Las Vegas altogether. Business was slowing down for both of them. The 1980's were basically a bridge between the post-mob 1970s and the corporate 1990s, where the larger properties worked hard to keep customers and some smaller properties closed. The hotels were turning a blind eye to girls working the lobbies, so out of town cathouses were not quite the same draw. Illegal bookmaking was coming under pressure in Las Vegas, and his connections to fights and races had dried up to the point he couldn't advantage bet at all.

A year to the day after the fire, Gina's mother had fallen ill and she had decided to head back to Minnesota; at first for a few weeks, which became a few months, then became indefinitely. The last phone call that Vig received from her was letting him know that she had sold the Salt Wells Villa, and that he would have to move his office out within a few weeks. She was sorry and appreciated him keeping an eye on the place, but that was that, she was staying at home for the foreseeable future.

Vig didn't resent the call. He just took the opportunity to make some changes himself. As well as the on-strip prices getting more competitive, a lot of the more forward-looking bookmakers were moving their businesses to the phone and basing them in Costa Rica. The infrastructure was acceptable, there was good flight connections, not too much corruption, the time zone was the same, and you could get American fast food. The locals all spoke English and Spanish, so you could hire a call center operative cheaply and quickly, and he would work hard and late if you paid him well. It was a good few years before the hedonistic online era, but the roots of a new industry were beginning to take hold.

One of the bookies working in an off-strip casino sportsbook told him that they were trying to hire line makers and telephone hosts to handle the whales that wanted to speak to Americans in their own accent. There were no traditional job advertisements; Vig gave his number to the bookie, who passed it on to their contact, and within a few days there was a message on his answering machine asking for him to callback with his mailing address. A few days later an open ticket from LAX to San Jose airport landed on his doorstep, with a handwritten note inviting him to meet the owner of the business at a specific address in San Jose any weekday at ten-o-clock in the morning.

There was nothing holding Vig back. Thirty-six hours later he was on a flight on his way for the first time to Costa Rica. He wondered if this was going to be a short visit or end up being an extended trip like his sojourn to Las Vegas all those years ago. He thought about staying for a few days beforehand, doing some reconnaissance, maybe finding out a little more about this business before he crossed the threshold, but in the end he got the cab directly from San Jose airport to the office address.

It didn't take long to get to the small nondescript building. The cab was not air conditioned so by the time he got there he was hot; he had taken off his jacket and loosened his collar and cuffs. There was no lobby or reception in the building, just a short hallway with a few small offices on one side and a pair of elevators on the other. The address said third floor; just as he hit the button to call the elevator, someone else walked into the building behind him. He seemed to be a tradesman; he was older than Vig, dressed in overalls and shirtless, and was pushing a trolley with what looked like five or six large desk partitions loaded on it – the kind that separate desks in open offices. As the doors on the elevator closed the tradesman turned and asked Vig in his strongly accented English whether he was going to meet "The Cigar", and Vig paused. Could it really be him?

When the elevator doors opened, Ronald 'The Cigar' Sacco was standing there himself to meet him. Vig found out later that he had a closed-circuit camera installed in the lobby that he could watch on one of the many TV's in his office. Vig wondered if it was an ambush, but the look on Sacco's face was warm, welcoming even.

"You made it. Glad to have you here, Vig."

Vig was cautious. There was a glass door through which he could see a mostly empty open-plan office. There were a few people seated at desks, and the guy who had travelled in the elevator with Vig had begun installing desk partitions as soon as he headed through the glass door. It didn't seem like a setup.

"It's certainly a surprise to see you. Nice that somebody who knows what they are doing is setting up one of these outfits."

Sacco smiled modestly.

"It's going to be a gold rush Vig. Some of the people

setting up down here don't know what they are doing, but I do. Set up a real office, wire it up right, hire the right mix of locals and Americans, and" – he pointed at Vig – "bring in people who really know what they are doing."

He gestured through the door.

"You ready to take some calls? I've got three phone lines so far and I'll make one exclusive to you. I'll pay you the same as the bookie's clerk in the I.P. – which will go a lot farther here – and five percent of the net hold on your top one-hundred monthly leads after deducting losses on the bottom hundred. I'll give you two months up front which we can take off at the end if you haven't paid it back out of your bonus by then. Get yourself an apartment."

This was what it was like in the early days of the telebetting business. If you were willing to bankroll an office and a good phone line you could get started, but Vig knew enough to know that the edge in this game was getting paid and getting a reputation for paying winners. It was here in Costa Rica that some bright spark came up with the idea of a local agent in the US with 'holding' bank accounts that would accept deposits and settlements and pay out winnings, and periodically wire the net hold to Costa Rica. Sacco had that side of things sewn up via some US front businesses. Sacco could even take Western Union payments over the phone via an agent who operated from the same building. He certainly was thorough.

Vig took his first call that very first day, on that single phone line, without even sitting down. What he brought to the table was his knowledge of the hosts, bookies and their clerks in the Las Vegas strip. If a caller told him that his main contact at Ceasers was 'Steve Cyr' then Vig knew this guy was a serious casino gambler with money. If he told him that he just bet at the window of any sportsbook he happened to be in, Vig knew he was 'NBD' – no big deal. If he said that he booked his sportsbook action directly with the main line maker, then Vig knew that he was a sharp.

Unlike some other bookies, Sacco's outfit welcomed sharps and used them to balance the book, making outbound calls if their book was out of line. Sharps always had money, kept it on account, and never complained about a bad result. Handling sharp bettors like this is why Sacco had brought in Vig.

And it was as simple as that. No big epiphany or big drama in their reunion. A man that Vig had run for his life from, was now his employer and colleague, and bygones were bygones. After the next few employees were hired Vig invested the last of his bankroll into the business for a clean ten points, under the table, and his salary-plus-bonus deal became salary-plus-bonus-plus-dividends. Vig and Sacco agreed to reinvest the dividends in the business point by point, until Vig's stake hit fifteen percent, at which point cash dividends would begin getting paid. Vig guessed that would take a couple of years but was a gamble with a lot of upside.

Sacco never even asked him anything about what had happened at the Benitez fight, or whether Gina was still in the picture, or anything that happened before he had showed up at the door of the office. He just paid Vig his nut and his nickel at the end of every month, and an extra slug of money on the weekends where they'd work together to balance a big line on the big games and races.

You wouldn't have called them friends, but their professional relationship extended beyond just the day-to-day boss-and-worker relationship. They watched and sweat ball games together on one of the four televisions Sacco had in his office specifically for that purpose. They shared a beer after work a couple of times a month, usually after a big event that they had either taken a bath in or taken a big haul.

Vig had been planning to quit around the time that Gina called the office. He had considered going back to Vegas, or to invest the last of his small roll in starting up a place of his own. But Gina arrived, and as usual, things changed.

39 GINA'S EPILOGUE

Minnesota

2nd November 1992

Dear Mr. Green,

We have not really met, but I feel that I know you. I saw you at Gina's funeral last month, and while the grief of my sister's untimely passing is still raw, a new grief for the life that she led out of her family's sight has come and almost overwhelmed me even more than her actual death.

As you can imagine, Gina's family never approved of the choices she made and the life she led, at least until she sold her business in Nevada. While her parents and I (I'm ten years older than her) disapproved, we were never surprised. From a very young age it was clear she was cut from a different cloth than the rest of the family. My father built our house in the 1950's and she was the first person to smoke a cigarette within its walls almost twenty years later. For most of that twenty years my father owned and maintained a car — his pride and joy — and she was the first one to take it out of state. Without permission, I might add. We only found out when the speeding tickets from Wisconsin arrived in the mail.

Gina always told me that she never worked as a working girl herself, and I believe her. She never lacked confidence or self-esteem, the usual crutches that lead to that sort of life. She worked in bars back west (yes, we still call it that) and one of them had a small establishment upstairs 'for regulars', and that is how she became familiar with the business side of vice. "The girls come and go, I try and make sure they leave in better shape than they arrive" she used to say. She couldn't talk to our parents about her plans to go into business herself, but she spoke to me. I think she felt that she would get the same disapproval from me but could at least have a civil conversation rather than an argument. I am crying now just thinking about that, I guess I was an older sister in some ways after all.

When friends and extended family asked what she was doing, we told them she had opened a laundry in a small town in Nevada. She had suggested we tell people that she had opened a bar or motel, but dad was afraid that if we told people that, they might be inclined to seek it out if they were in the area. I have no doubt that some of the local men have visited that part of the country and found out that the 'Wilson Launderette' was in fact the 'Salt Wells Villa' but they weren't bringing it up in church meetings or anywhere else, and are certainly not bringing it up now.

It was always a joy when Gina came to visit. Above all else her parents and myself all knew that she was happy. I'm not sure exactly how or when she met you, she described you as the 'gentleman who she took to see Sinatra' so I assume you met at a show or casino. She was always very careful to tell us that you were not a degenerate gambler, not a 'john' (her words), and not a liability.

She didn't talk about you every trip home, but when she told us she always made it clear you were one-of-a-kind. She seemed afraid of losing your companionship. I never asked her was she in love with you, but all I can say as her big sister was that if she ever loved anyone in that way, it was you. The only other person she loved was her son Jack Junior. I don't know if she ever told you about her son. She had him at fifteen, with a boy — Jack - who was barely her friend let alone her boyfriend. The father's parents were young and had a young family themselves, so offered to take in Jack Junior to live with them. They never hid the fact that the child was really a grandchild (who would call two brothers by the same name?) but raised him as their own. Gina was eternally grateful, and never sought to reestablish her parenthood, knowing on some level that Jack Junior was getting all the love and care — and sibling companionship — he would need.

Unfortunately, poor Jack Junior only made it to his tenth birthday before he was taken by bad pneumonia and a weak heart. Jacks' father was a doctor and did everything he could to get him well, and when the time came he did everything he could to make the child comfortable. Gina always visited Jack Junior, but was not there at the very end, something she always regretted. She never — to my knowledge — visited his grave apart from one time shortly after he was buried.

I don't know if this explains why she was the way she was. She believed that she was lucky she hadn't tried to raise him herself, as she was spared this grief, as our late mother was spared Gina's untimely passing.

I hope this letter fills some of the gaps, or answers some questions, or explains things. I am not writing for any other reason than I feel you have spent enough time with her especially in the later years to have a right to know these things.

I don't expect a response but please know that you are always welcome to visit at the Wilson home.

Sincerely,

Violet Wilson

PS Thank you for the coffee beans. I still cannot believe that Gina grew them on her own coffee farm!

40 PHONE CALL

January 2nd, 1986

"Hi, how can I direct your call?"

"Hi Carole, it's Vig."

"Vig! Long time no speak. How are you doing?"

"Oh, so-so. Is the boss in?"

"Mr. S?"

"Mr. S."

"Yes, he is. He's not in a good mood, Vig. I hope you have some good news for him."

"Thanks for the tip, Carole."

(a pause)

"Vig."

"Hey Ron, you got five minutes to talk?"

"Exactly five for you Vig. If you are looking for money, you have less."

"I'll cut to the chase then. I have a business proposition for you."

No reply, just the sound of a cigar being lit.

"I have a problem I need solved. Not my usual kind of problem."

"I take it this is my type of problem?"

"Yes, I guess it is."

"I don't do that stuff anymore, Vig."

"I have two casual employees up here in Doka, in my coffee plantation."

"You weren't kidding."

"I wasn't."

"Go on."

"Those employees are presenting me a workforce problem. Basically, they are running a side business on my property, and putting my staff to work for them on the side."

"And what's in it for me?"

"My share. Free and clear."

"The whole lot?" He paused. "That's the short end of the deal for you, if you don't mind me saying. Unless these two guys are connected locally. They're not, are they?"

"They're not."

"How decisively do you need this problem solved."

"I leave that up to you. I want them away from my property, and preferably out of the country. They are related to some of the other staff, so I want them to leave of their own volition."

"Of their own volition." Another pause. "Where would these guys be typically found during the working day?"

"South west corner of Doka. Not far from the back gate we seldom use. You know where I mean?"

"No, but I know people who will know."

"You will help me?"

"Two weeks' maximum. Possibly less. I normally would shake on a deal like this, but I guess that's not an option?"

"We can shake after. Come up and visit the plantation. The coffee is great."

"I might just do that. Call me in two weeks."

(click)

41 SHERI'S

2580 Highland Drive Las Vegas
February 18th 1986

Vig was sitting in the main showroom of Sheri's Cabaret, at one of the small tables two rows from the stage. There were two empty seats beside him, but the rest of the joint was full. A reserved sign on the table kept the occasional seat-hunter away. The music had just re-started; some low and slow electric guitar in a repeating melody, that drifted on for a couple of minutes. The MC spoke quietly into the microphone.

"Now gentlemen... Sheri's is pleased to bring you... the double-act you've all been waiting for... Misty Green and Misty Blue."

There was a polite ripple of applause from the crowd. Most of the patrons were men, but there were a few couples dotted around at private tables, and one table was three girls and one older man. The dancers did not emerge for a few minutes, while the guitar intro played. The intro was long, and the crowd was patient.

Oh it's been too many times and I can't go back
Night bars, guitars, rundown motels like shacks

192

What it mounts up to I don't want it at all
Lost you and I want you today

As the first verse played softly, dry ice and smoke filled the stage, and two willowy figures entered from either side of the stage. They were the same height, and both had short cropped hair. The two girls were local and had started dancing in nineteen-seventy-eight when U.F.O. had come to Carson City. They were both called Misty and had been inspired by the song to become a double act. It was a good goddamn song.

This were unlike your typical strip club or brothel cabaret fayre. Their dance was subtle, unhurried, and was not directed at the audience. Their moves were not coordinated, and they did they show any awareness of the other's presence on the stage. It was as if they were each dancing alone. They both moved slowly downstage and the dance became more focused.

Misty green and blue
Love to love to love you
Misty green and blue
Love to love to love you

Just as the first verse ended a figure approached Vig's table and took the seat directly to his left. He was expecting the three of them to come together, but it was just Sacco. The two dancers had made their way to the center of the stage and were dancing close, face-to-face.

"Vig."

"Ron."

"They are on their way. You sure you want to be here?"

"Yes."

Vig wanted to be there to face them in person. Sacco had offered to get the truth and deal with the situation, but Vig had to be one hundred percent sure before things got out of hand.

To be something, to be near you
Don't say that you'll never know

Love to love to love you

The stage had darkened, and the two girls were still dancing in their own individual but overlapping spotlights. The house lights were completely off, the only light in the audience was from the candles on each table, and the occasional spark of a cigarette being lit. The audience had gone completely quiet.

There was a door just behind and to the left of Vig's table; he heard it being pushed open and muffled voices come in the door. He turned around slowly and saw three figures approach in a close huddle towards the table, two abreast.

Sacco didn't turn around. "Here's our guest now."

He sat down. For a coffee-picker he had scrubbed up well... it was surprising to see a drug dealing bootlegger had a sports-jacket and clean shoes.

Sacco read Vig's mind. "We turned him out nicely for the occasion, Vig." He nodded to the two standing figures who withdrew into the shadows. They gave the impression that they were not going too far.

Half the time it could seem funny
The other half is just too sad
This west bound moon's only rise and fall
Lost you and I want you today

He hadn't spoken since they sat down, but the nervousness was palpable. Sacco reached into his pocket and there was a flash of polished steel. They both jumped, but it was only a cigar cutter and cigar, which Sacco ceremoniously cut and lit at the table, still never turning his head from the stage.

By this point the show had become a lot more... not explicit, but intimate. The audience were not seeing any additional skin, but the way that Misty Green and Misty Blue danced made you feel like a voyeur, like you were seeing something taboo and private.

Misty green and blue

Love to love to love you
Misty green and blue
Love to love to love you

For a moment, it seemed like Sacco had forgotten where he was, but as quickly as the moment came, it vanished. He turned to face the man and spoke over the music "You are Ramon Estrada, yes?"

Ramon nodded.

"You know who he is?"

He nodded again, without taking his gaze off Sacco.

There was an edge in Sacco's voice "Look again. Be certain. You know who he is?"

Ramon and Sacco both glanced at Vig, who didn't dare to look back at him. Would he see bruises and cuts, or just terror? He nodded again.

Sacco's voice again. "Victor, you recognize Ramon?"

"Yes."

Sacco nodded to himself "Okay, so we are clear as to who everyone is. Now you are going to tell la jefe here exactly why you think you are here."

The music reached a crescendo – wailing guitars and thrashing drums where words were no longer apparently enough. Ramon didn't speak.

Sacco looked disappointed. There was an almost imperceptible move of his head, and suddenly and silently out of the darkness his two henchmen stepped forward. The first, the larger of the two, put his hands firmly on Ramon's shoulders, and in the same movement the second henchman had grabbed Ramon's arm and pressed it down flat palm-up on the table.

To be something, to be near you
I don't know where I'm goin' to
I've tried and I need you to stay

Before Vig could react, Sacco had gently pressed the lit end of the cigar against Ramon's wrist, and as he did this the first henchman had put his gloved hand over his mouth. His brief scream was muffled and drowned out by the music.

Sacco was calm "Hablar. Ahora. O te pones encendida como mi cigarro."

"Gusano!" Sacco was dragging on his cigar to get it relit. A few coals were still smoldering on Ramon's wrist. The two henchmen had not loosened their grip.

Ramon broke his silence. "Por favor! No tome nada. Nada!"

Sacco snapped "English."

Ramon turned to Vig. "I'm sorry jefe. I didn't steal anything. The still was already there, we didn't think we were doing any harm."

Sacco looked at Vig but spoke to Ramon.

"So, tell him what you were doing."

"We were just making Maté, just a little to bottle and sell. Not alcohol or anything."

Sacco spoke to me. "You satisfied Vig?"

Vig looked at Ramon, who looked terrified. He knew better than to show any sympathy. "I'm satisfied."

Sacco seemed satisfied too. He sat back in his chair and took a draw from his cigar. He raised his hand and motioned to a waiter, who took a few seconds to appear. He ordered three highballs without asking what the others wanted. As the drinks arrived the song finished, the two girls vanishing out of the spotlight into the darkness.

Ramon seemed to relax a little. "Am... am I fired?"

Sacco turned his entire body slowly around to look at him. At first his face was serious, but after a moment a smile broke across his face. The smile turned into a grin, and then a laugh. He began to laugh hysterically.

Ramon was nonplussed. The stage was now empty.

Sacco leaned towards us conspiratorially and winked "You want to meet the girls?"

Without waiting for an answer, he nodded to the nearby waiter. "Three more drinks, and a bottle of champagne on ice for the girls. Send the drinks back, we'll join them shortly."

After a few minutes, the three of them headed backstage through a small unmarked door at the side of the stage. It opened to a narrow corridor, with another door that had a large security guard with a cowboy hat standing outside it.

"The girls are expecting you, Mister Sacco."

The door opened. Vig didn't know what he would see, a lit mirror, a rack of costumes maybe. It was a bare room with two benches and a couple of stools. The two girls sat side by side, with what appeared to be men's shirts over their 'stage clothes', both smoking cigarettes. On one of the stools was the tray of drinks, and there was an empty glass on the floor that seemed to have been used as an ashtray.

The girls looked at the three men as they stood there inside the door, without speaking. To Vig it seemed like ten minutes but was probably more like fifteen seconds. It was strange; two girls sitting down smoking, clearly had the upper hand on the three more-or-less burly ne'er do well gentlemen that were standing before them. Vig could not imagine what was going through Ramon's head, he didn't seem to have an inkling what would happen next.

Blue eventually spoke. "Which one of you sent the champagne?"

Sacco smiled "That was me. We're celebrating my friend Ramon's birthday."

"Well, happy birthday Ramon!" Blue spoke as the two girls stood up and walked towards them. She looked at Green who smiled back at her. "Perhaps we need to give him an extra special birthday present?"

They beckoned to Ramon to take a seat on one of the empty stools. Vig looked at Sacco, and he looked right back at him dead in the eyes. "Grab your drink, Vig. This should be quite a show."

Ramon – seemingly oblivious to the strangeness of the situation – sat down. Green handed him her cigarette – a joint as it turned out – and sat down on his lap. She didn't sit astride him like a stripper or a whore, she sat on him like he was Santa

Claus. She took the joint from his mouth and took a long drag and handed it to Blue who stood behind him. The scene was surreal – no music, no words, Ramon was silent, but seemed to be relaxed.

Sacco was leaning against the door watching the scene unfold. Vig suspected he was ensuring that nobody tried to leave. Vig had briefly considered making a run for it.

Green put her hands gently on Ramon's shoulders and whispered something into his ear, too low for Vig or Sacco to hear. Ramon smiled, and Green handed him his drink. Blue was still sitting relatively modestly on his lap and was smiling herself between drags on her own cigarette. She looked up at Green and smiled and began slowly unbuttoning Ramon's shirt. As she undid each button, Green pulled the shirt down around his shoulders exposing his vest. By the time the shirt was down around his elbows, both joints were finished, and Ramon could no longer lift his hand up to bring his drink to his mouth.

"Hey girls, let me take it off?"

As soon as he spoke the expression on Green's face changed. She had been twisting the shirt around behind his back and now twisted it quickly around twice more, trapping Ramon's arms behind his back. Time seemed to slow down. Vig stood stock still, half expecting one of them to produce a weapon. What happened was a lot more prosaic; Blue reached back with her balled up fist and simply punched him across the jaw, and as she did Green tipped the chair back with his arms trapped behind and let him fall to the floor. Blue didn't leave his lap, just pivoting onto the floor on top of him. Two more quick hits to the bridge of his nose and he still had no idea where he was. Green had produced something clear, like Saran wrap, and while Blue kept sitting on him Green began to place it over Ramon's face. As soon as it was over his head Blue dropped one more quick punch to his chest, which made him exhale rapidly, and when he tried to inhale the bag prevented him, the plastic almost ballooning into his mouth and filling it. Green began to wrap Ramon's head, slowly and carefully.

Ramon struggled but with his hands trapped behind him in his tightened shirt, and both girls holding him down, so it was futile.

While this was happening, Sacco didn't move, and his eyes hadn't left Vig, who looked at him while barely holding his composure. He would rather look at Sacco than at the grisly tableau in the middle of the room.

The noises abated.

Sacco turned slightly and knocked gently on the door behind him. The henchman and the cowboy bouncer were right outside and had clearly been waiting for the signal. They walked in barely acknowledging the standing men or the girls, still on the floor now breathing heavily with exertion. Henchman had what looked like a large toweling bedsheet with him, which he simply lay on the floor beside the prone body of Ramon.

Blue stood up and casually picked up the bottle of champagne from the bucket and used it to gesture towards the door. "OK if we go?"

Sacco nodded, and they split. By the time they were gone the body was wrapped in the towel. He was small, so the two easily carried him between them. They didn't even ask… they just left just a few moments after the girls. Just like that; within ten minutes of coming into the room, Vig and Sacco were alone.

"Job done, Vig. He won't be found in our lifetime. He will be buried with someone else who we have been keeping on ice just for a situation like this. You see, when two people are found, the cops will assume their deaths are related. If – and it's a big if – he is found, they'll assume that he was involved with the small-time La Brea homo moneylender he is buried with. Don't bother telling me that this is not what you wanted, or this is not what you expected. I solved the problem as you needed. Okay?".

42 ADIOS

After Sheri's, Vig had stayed in Nevada for a few months until he was sure things had died down. He called Gina and told her what had happened. He didn't trust the privacy of the Costa Rican phone lines, so he called her from his old office in Pahrump where the phones were at least somewhat secure. There had been almost no gossip at the plantation; the other staff knew that Ramon was a fuck up and were happy to see him fired.

A few months later, after money had come in from the harvest and the staff and bills had been paid, Gina flew up to Vegas to meet Vig. They checked into a motel and kept a low profile. Gina had lived and worked on the fringes of the Nevada experience, and the occasional disappearance was part of that experience, but this was the closest either of them had come to something like this.

"I don't get why it had to happen here, and why you had to be there?"

It was the obvious question, and Vig had put the same one to Sacco, who was very matter of fact. He knew exactly how to adios a body in Nevada, who to speak to, who to trust, and the palms that need to be greased. In Costa Rica he had a legitimate business that was becoming more and more subject to scrutiny, and less people willing to do 'wet work' that he could rely on. So Vegas it was.

They were standing by the ice machine in the motel when Vig was recounting the story to Gina.

She was sanguine. "So now we go back to making coffee, Vig?"

"Now we go back to making coffee." He dropped the bucket into the ice. "You fancy the two-week road trip, or the flight?

NOTES AND REFERENCES

Chapter 1: 'The Las Vegas Experts Gambling Guide'
The guide written by Robert Scharff was published in 1968 and was one of the first gambling guides that did not just shill for the casinos. It has more wisdom in the single chapter *'How to Survive (and Sometimes Prosper)'* than most gambling books have in their entirety. It admits the long run is inevitable but acknowledges the short run can be fun.

Chapter 1: Pahrump
Another famous sign hung above the archway leading to the bedrooms of the Chicken Ranch and read "Walking the minimum gets you fired". It was to remind the girls that while they could negotiate extras with the clients, they couldn't reject those who just wanted the basics.

Chapter 1: Circus-Circus
On the dates that Vig checked into the Circus, there was no hotel. Opening without a hotel meant that the Circus could not attract and retain high rollers. When twenty-three million dollars was borrowed from the Teamsters, they installed Tony Spilotro to control the local organized crime interests (including the skim at the Circus) under the name of Tony Stuart, operating out of a gift concession on the premises.

Chapter 1: Prostitution in Vegas
Under Nevada law, any county with a population of seven hundred thousand people is allowed to have licensed brothels. This means Clark County - which contains Las Vegas - is excluded. This limit has been periodically increased as the other counties have grown.

Chapter 2: Sidney Poitier
In Neil Simon's memoir "Rewrites" he described Sidney Poitier as a person who took his poker and tennis very seriously. The story of the marker is fictional.

Chapter 2: The Brush
Poker rooms have a 'brush' to keep tables and waiting lists balanced, and the position is named after the small brush they used to hold to clean up the table felt. It is a separate role to the floorman, but in smaller rooms (or

during quieter times) the roles can be done by one person

Chapter 2: Past-Posting
Past-posting is simply placing a bet after the result is known.

Chapter 2: Casino Chips
Casino chips of significant value ($5,000 or more) are nowadays tracked with computer chips so that casinos know where they are played – and if rumors are to be believed – where they are being held in the property. Back in the nineteen-sixties they were just big brown chips made of pressed clay. It was very common in Las Vegas for casinos to exchange each other's chips. The upside for the casino doing this was getting the play from competitors, and they could simply exchange them at face value every few days. As well as that, restaurants, strip clubs, and call girls also treated them like currency. The only time this caused a problem was when there was a heist and the chip design had to be changed, or just before a casino closed.

Chapter 3: Beryl Cameron-Gibbons
Beryl Cameron-Gibbons was one of the first women in the world to be granted a boxing promoters license. Based in London, she was the owner of the "Thomas A' Beckett", above which all the boxing greats (including Sugar Ray Leonard) sparred in at some point. There is no indication she ever travelled to or lived in the United States or got involved in any 'gambling parties' as described. All events depicted are fictional.

Chapter 3: Jack Binion
Jack Binion became president of his father's Horseshoe casino and became synonymous with the game of poker when he developed the World Series of Poker in 1970.

Chapter 4: The Martingale System
Every gambler invents the Martingale. They figure they have a way to beat the casinos at their own game and cannot believe that nobody thought of it before. It's a simple progressive-stake betting system, where you double your bet after each loss. The idea is that you only need to win once to make your initial bet as profit. Bet five dollars on black; if you win, you're five bucks up and you are done. If you lose, you are five dollars down, so just bet ten the next time. If you win, you've got your five back, and your five profit; done. You can keep doubling your bet, and eventually you will most certainly hit black, and be a whole five dollars up. I won't bore you with the math, but

basically you almost always win five, and occasionally lose everything. The frequent 'fives' don't add up to the infrequent 'everything', so it's a system strictly for suckers. The suckers assume that the maximum bets on each table are to protect themselves against martingalers... the reality is that they really love people putting their entire roll on the line every time just to win a tiny amount.

Chapter 5: Poker Game

The poker between Vig, Art, Aileen, Benny and the others is entirely fictional. Art was of the most famous boxers in Los Angeles in the early fifties, a celebrity in the Hollywood Legion and the Olympic Stadium. He regularly mixed with celebrities including Marilyn Monroe and William Holden. Aileen was indeed the "Queen of the West Coast"; the biggest boxing promoter of the time and controlled most of the boxing action in California in the 1950's. Benny was a contemporary and friend of Art Aragon. It is not known if he played poker... but with a name like that it's easy to imagine he did.

Chapter 5: John Scarne and the Scarne Riffle

John Scarne was the mechanic's mechanic. He learned how to manipulate cards at a very young age. He was hired as a consultant by the United States army to educate soldiers about the dangers of card sharps, who were rife at the front lines in the second world war. He developed a very effective shuffling method that he christened - in his usual self-aggrandizing way - the "Scarne Riffle". He was notorious for his attempted discrediting of blackjack card counting systems... this author believes that this was motivated by his employment by the Las Vegas casinos.

Chapter 6: Blackjack and 'Playing off the Card'

Playing 'off the card' is playing close to perfect blackjack strategy. For every set of blackjack rules there is a way to play perfectly, keeping the dealer's edge under one percent. A card-counter can improve that edge, an advantage player can improve it even more.

Chapter 7: Dave Swan

The entertainer came from Wales to Las Vegas as a comedian in 1979. He estimated that he performed over twenty thousand times on the Las Vegas Strip. He was the first comic ever to walk onstage at the Imperial and the Stratosphere, and the last comic ever to work the Copa Room at the Sands. He played King Arthur in the Excalibur Casino's 'Tournament of Kings' until his death in 2008. Before his death, fellow Las Vegas entertainers staged a benefit concert at the Imperial Palace to help with his medical costs.

Chapter 7: Tony
Tony was a barman at the Imperial Palace in the 1980s and later settled down in the Isle of Man in the British Isles, spending his days golfing and driving around the local gamblers and poker enthusiasts in his taxicab. The conversations with Vig are all fictional.

Chapter 8: Odds
For the non-American readers, a quick explanation of odds terminology. Odds of 'minus four-hundred' mean that you must bet $400 to win back $500 total. In Britain they would call that 'one to four' or 'four to one on' and an Asian gambler would call it 'one-point-two-five'. Conversely, odds of 'plus three-hundred' mean that your $100 bet will win $400 total. Sugar Ray Leonard was indeed a 3 to 1 (-300 / 1.33) favorite in the Benitez fight.

Chapter 8: Rafael Benitez
Benitez was a legendary fighter; he took on multiple belts at multiple weights and won most of them. There is no way he threw the Sugar Ray Leonard fight or any other professional boxing match as suggested in this book. However, his own father wrote an article in the November article of 'The Ring' entitled "Why Benitez Won't Win" which included the phrase 'he would rather be out anywhere rather than the ring'.

Chapter 8: The Palomino and Cervantes Fights
At age seventeen while still in school, Benitez faced WBA Light Welterweight champion Antonio Cervantes (better known as "Kid Pambele") in his eleventh lineal title defense. Benitez won and then defended three times. He then took on WBC World Champion Carlos Palomino, and won. The fight on November 30th 1979 was his second attempt at a defense.

Chapter 9: Hillcrest Country Club
In the early days of Hollywood, Jews were not permitted to join the majority of country clubs, so instead they joined Hillcrest. It counted many of Hollywood's biggest stars amongst its membership, including Milton Berle, Jack Benny, Danny Kaye, George Burns, Louis B. Mayer, Sam Goldwyn, and the Marx Brothers. Country clubs were funny about who used the pool. Groucho himself was offered a membership in at least one other club as long as his family agreed to never use the pool.

Chapter 9: Carmine

Carmine E Yanuck is based on Daryl F Zanuck, who did indeed lose his studio in a hostile takeover by his own family (including his son, Richard). Every other aspect of the story - including his involvement in gambling - is fictional.

Chapter 11: Gina Wilson

Gina Wilson (real name, Reina Fuchigami) was the madam of the Salt Wells Villa between 1975 and 1980. Apart from her proprietorship of the Villa, her entire story here is fictional.

Chapter 11: The Salt Wells Villa

The Salt Wells Villa was a legal brothel in Churchill County, Nevada between 1975 and 2004. It was famously firebombed by the local Sheriff's wife in 1977; she pled guilty and was incarcerated briefly. Gina Wilson gave up control in 1980, and the premises was subsequently sold to a bowling-alley owner from Illinois who would charge the sailors from the local Naval Air Station on their government-issued credit cards as "James Fine Dining". After that, things went downhill.

Chapter 11: Casino Hosts

Before Southwest Airlines cut the price of airfares all over the west coast, the rich whales were brought from Los Angeles to Las Vegas by hosts, who would have them collected from their California homes or hotels and brought to the door of their favorite casino. The host ensured the whale got the best deals on comps, and the casino paid the host a percentage of their total action (usually the handle, not the hold).

Chapter 12: The Other Place

The Other Place was a gay bar operated by Marge Jacques. The description of the interior is correct, but the story of bookmaker taking up residence there after hours, is entirely fictional.

Chapter 13: The Labouchere System

The Labouchere system is – like the Martingale – a system designed for gamblers with a specific bankroll who want to hit a specific winning amount. It has the benefit of looking easy and infallible but requiring some paperwork, so you feel smart doing it. You write down a list of numbers totaling your desired win. You bet the sum of the first and last number on a fifty-fifty proposition; if you win you cross the numbers off, if you lose you add the total to the list. Repeat till broke or you hit your target. I'm not going to bother explaining why this is a road to nowhere other than to say there's a lot of systems that promise a small win most of the time and a big loss rarely, and this is yet another one of them.

Chapter 18: Ronald Sacco

Ronald "The Cigar" Sacco was one of the first, and ostensible most famous, bookmakers to ever serve U.S bettors. As well as apparently being a founder and key person for BetCris in Costa Rica, he did some jail time for various gambling activities from the early seventies. The adventure at Ceasers Palace and the work he did with Vig in Costa Rica, is entirely fictional.

Chapter 19: Jeorg

Jeorg is based on a real person and the story is a real story. If he's reading this, he knows who he is.

Chapter 23: Craps

Craps is a simple game designed for people to bet against each other, that the casino business took and changed to make it a game played against the house. When it was played on the streets and in backroom games, it was a simple game where the player holding the dice decided how much he was willing to bet, and the others at the game offered to fade the bets. The roller would win ('pass') 49.3% of the time, the faders would win ('don't pass') 50.7% of the time. When the game moved into casinos, they couldn't offer such good don't-pass odds, so they crippled that bet by making one roll in thirty-six a push (usually the twelve, occasionally the two), and making the pass line much more attractive by offering true odds on subsequent number bets once you had gone beyond one roll. Every time you rolled a number that didn't win or lose, then you could bet with zero vig on that number coming up again before a seven and keep rolling and adding numbers while you dodged that unlucky seven-out. The "field" is one of the sucker bets, but thankfully the Trop likes to pay triple on sixes and double on ones, keeping the vig down to 2.8%.

Chapter 23: Three Card Monte and Rod the Hop

One of the most famous purveyors of this game was Roderick William Dee, known as 'Rod the Hop' who plied the trade from the seventies to his death in 2013. The following are Rod's own words on three card monte, reproduced from bobarno.com:

"Believe it or not, all you have to do is set up a box and start throwing cards and people will just stop by to see what you're doing. You don't have to say anything. Then you start betting with the shills. And pretty soon people get to realize that it's a betting game. I'll keep throwing it, and my shills will be betting, and they'll be winning, and the sucker sees them winning, and so they want to bet. And I might even let the sucker win some if I see other suckers that might have more money.

So, the red card is on the bottom of the two cards and the black card is on top. When I throw the cards down, I'll throw the top card instead of the bottom card, which is the red card. But first, just to get into the rhythm of it, I'll do it for real. I'll throw the red card on the bottom, and let them watch where it is, very slowly, and they're watching and wondering where the red card is. And there's no question where the red card is.

And they'll want to bet, so I'll say, well here, let me do it again. And then I'll pick them up and they'll say, oh gosh, I was right. I knew where the red card was. And then I'll do it again, and now they'll want to bet. When I don't want them to win is when I'll throw the top cards. And then obviously they'll lose.

You would think that a normal person would think, wait a minute, I knew where the red card was. I bet on it and I lost. Why? Well you'd think a guy would just quit. But no, not suckers. Suckers go, 'wait, this time I'm really going to watch him.' And then they'll bet more money, and it just goes on and on until they don't have any more money. So, I try to entice as many suckers as I can to bet on it. Then, when everybody's out of money, I take the cards, stick them in my pocket, and walk away."

Chapter 23: The sale of the Tropicana

The Tropicana was part of a large skimming operation in 1978, where money was siphoned from the cage to the Kansas City mob. It was exposed in 1979 and the owners were forced to sell to the Ramada Inns corporation. There is no evidence that any of their floormen arranged a final heist before they closed.

Chapter 25: Barnett Magids

The FBI suspected that the first Clay / Liston fight in nineteen-sixty-four may have been fixed by the mob. Ash Resnick was a local Vegas personality with links to the Genovese family, allegedly cleared over a million dollars on the fight despite an article in Sports Illustrated suggesting the exact opposite. The person who allegedly sang to the FBI was Barnett Magids. His part in the airstrip heist is entirely fictional.

Chapter 25: Ralph Engelstad

Ralph Englestad was the owner of the Imperial Palace and later the Klondike Casinos in Las Vegas. He was one of the very few non-corporate affiliated owners in Vegas. The Ralph Engelstad Arena at the University of North Dakota was named after its major donor, and he was also involved in developing the Las Vegas Motor Speedway. While he did host Nazi-themed parties, and owned the Thunderbird airstrip, nothing else here involving baseball, counterfeit money, or the Ramada Group actually happened.

Chapter 26: The Pacifica
It was the HoJo in the mid-seventies, the Paradise for a couple of years, then the Twentieth Century, then the Treasury, then the Pacifica, and until very recently was a Hooters, serving half-table craps and boneless wings twenty-four hours a day.

Chapter 27: The Wedding
This is a true story, at least as true as any story. The two survivors were reportedly men from the wedding party, not father and daughter. There is no connection to Ralph Engelstad or any other characters in this book. From the New York Times dated March 19th 1911;

"Tragic details of the fate of a wedding party attacked by wolves in Asiatic Russia while driving on sledges to the bride's house, where a banquet was to have taken place, are now at hand, and in their ghastly reality surpass anything ever imagined by a fiction writer. The exceptionally severe weather has been the cause of many minor tragedies in which the wolves have played a part, but perhaps none has ever been known so terrible as that now reported, since in this instance no fewer than 118 persons are said to have perished.

A wedding party numbering 120 persons set out in thirty sledges to drive twenty miles from the village of Obstipoff to Tashkend. The ground was thickly covered with snow, and the progress was necessarily delayed, but the greater part of the journey was accomplished in safety. At a distance of a few miles from Tashkend the horses suddenly became restive, and the speculation of the travelers changed to horror when they discerned a black cloud moving rapidly toward them across the snowfield. Its nearer approach showed it to be composed of hundreds of wolves, yelping furiously, and evidently frantic with hunger, and within a few seconds the hindmost sledges were surrounded. Panic seized the party, and those in the van whipped up the horses and made desperate attempts to escape, regardless of their companions, but the terrified horses seemed almost incapable of movement.

A scene frightful almost beyond description was now enacted. Men, women and children, shrieking with fear, defended themselves with whatever weapons they could, but to no avail, and one after another fell amidst the snarling beasts. The wolves, roused still further by the taste of blood, rushed toward the leading sledges, and though the first dozen conveyances managed to stave them off for a time, it was only at a terrible cost, since it is asserted that the women occupants were thrown out to be devoured by the animals. The pursuit, however, never slackened, and the carnage went on until only the foremost sledge—that containing the bride and the bridegroom—remained beyond the wolves' reach. A nightmare race was kept up for a few hundred yards, and it seemed as though the danger was being evaded, when suddenly a fresh pack of wolves appeared.

The two men accompanying the bridal couple demanded that the bride should be sacrificed, but the bridegroom indignantly rejected the cowardly proposition, whereupon the men seized and overpowered the pair and threw them out to a horrible fate. Then they succeeded in rousing their horses to a last effort, and, though attacked in turn, beat off the wolves and eventually reached Tashkend, the only two survivors of the happy party which had set out from Obstipoff. Both men were in a semi-demented state from their experience."

Chapter 27: The Battle of Vilnius
The battle for Vilnius and Reiner Stahl's leadership happened more or less exactly as Ralph described, and made a significant impact on the Red Army's movement west. His family's involvement is entirely fictional.

Chapter 28: Sonny Brunson and Bruce Abbitt
In September 1979, Sonny Brunson and Bruce Abbitt purchased hundred-dollar bill photographic plates from Richard Howard, allegedly because Brunson needed front money for a drug deal. They printed the bills at the Insty-Print. On October 2nd 1979 Brunson was arrested. In Sonny's apartment was found a booklet entitled "The How's and Why's of the Counterfeiter".

Chapter 30: Mike Fererro
Mike Ferrero was a moderately successful ball player in the seventies but became famous during game two of the series. In the eighth inning, Willie Randolph singled, and with two outs Bob Watson ripped a liner to deep left field. Ferraro waved Randolph home, but hadn't counted on George Brett dropping to pick up Willie Wilson's overthrow and then spinning to throw Randolph out at the plate. The Royals ended up winning the game 3–2 and the owner George Steinbrenner fired Ferraro at the end of the season. There is no evidence or even rumors that he ever took a bribe or called him home on purpose. Avron Fogelman bought the team a couple of years after the events described in this book. Howser refused to fire Mike Ferraro, so Stienbrenner fired Howser. Kansas City did go on to hire Howser to manage the last part of the short 1981 season, and he went on to finish runner up the following two years and rebuild the team in time to take the division title in 1984 and the World Series in 1985. There is no suggestion that Ferrero's wave home was intentional or corrupt.

Chapter 33: The Silverleaf
The Silverleaf claimed to be the smallest bar in St Louis. Open since the fifties, it certainly had the smallest bathrooms and prices. More notably, during the 80's it had a jukebox with no music recorded after 1976.

Chapter 34: Empeys / Barbary Coast / Bills / Cromwell
The Barbary Coast in its various incarnations was an almost-perfect metaphor for the changes that had happened in the new end of the strip. As 'Empeys Desert Villa' it had been a simple modern motel, boasting for many years on the sign out front that it was "Brand New. Every Convenience. Pool. TV. Phones.". It was a place to stay and take a break from the more hectic parts of Las Vegas. When the desert-racer Michael Gaughan bought the place in 1979 he built the hotel and casino that more-or-less still exists today, with the iconic brightly lit entrance. In the 1990s one of the hippest nightspots in town (Drai's) ran alongside the fattest Elvis Presley impersonator in town (Pete Vallee), a contradiction that made sense only to those who knew and loved the Barbary Coast, and reflected the eternal swirl of the tacky and the slick, the old-fashioned and the new-fangled, and the slacks-and-shorts and the cocktail dress, that had become modern Las Vegas. The absorption of this property into the Harrah conglomerate in 2007 removed a lot of its beauty (notably the beautifully lit signage seen on the book cover) and some of its spirit, but it remains a pretty nice oasis at one of the busiest parts of the strip, and is the author's favorite place to stay.

Chapter 34: The old MGM
The MGM referred to in the story is the old one where Bally's is now, not the new one at the other end of the strip. At the time of the fire, approximately 5,000 people were on the property. It broke out at 7.05am in the Deli, then spread across the areas of the casino in which no fire sprinklers were installed, and a few minutes after the whole casino was engulfed, a huge fireball blew out the frontage onto the street. Seventy-seven people died from smoke and / or carbon monoxide, three from burns and smoke inhalation, one from burns, and one from jumping from a high window. Six hundred and fifty people were injured.

Chapter 34: The Sunrise Hospital
Earlier that year, one nurse had been indicted, and seven other staff were suspended at the Surnrise Hospital; it was believed they were taking bets on when patients would die. The nurse Jani Adams was eventually cleared, but it was one of the biggest stories in Las Vegas that year, at least until the MGM fire.

Chapter 35: BetCris and Costa Rica
The address given is the approximate location of the offices of BetCris, one of the early US-facing Costa Rica based sportsbooks. It went online in 1995

but was established as a telebetting operation in 1985.

Chapter 35: Doka

A working coffee farm since 1908, the Vargas family have been growing coffee in the Doka estate for more than 100 years. As far as this author is aware, they have never sold.

Chapter 41: Sheri's

Sheri's (now closed) was one of the most upscale nude bars in Las Vegas. It was famous for its more traditional cabaret feel, with a proper stage and seating, and a well-tended dry bar with a liquid backdrop.

ACKNOWLEDGMENTS

Barry Carter and Rick Dacey for encouragement and advice.

Lee Jones and Deke Castleman for reading the early drafts.

Rosalind for editing and proofing.

ABOUT THE BOOK

This is a work of fiction. The character of Vig is fiction. The rest of the characters are loosely based on real people, with fictional elements added.

The "Notes and References" section gives details of where the truth deviates from the story.

ABOUT THE AUTHOR

David Lyons developed a keen interest in gambling while training as an actuary. He has worked in gambling and poker for over a decade. While currently based in Ireland, much of this book has been written while travelling between the Isle of Man, Malta, Costa Rica, Plovdiv, Las Vegas and Perth.